**Patri**

MW01025722

# Mirror Mirror

*A Jack Dillon Dublin tale...*

ISBN # 13: 978-1979365420

ISBN# 10: 1979365423

# **Acknowledgments**

I would like to thank the following

people for their help & support:

Special thanks to Nick, Paul, Roy, Julie, Mittie, and Toui for their hard work, cheerful patience and positive feedback. I would like to thank family and friends for their encouragement and unqualified support. Special thanks to Maggie, Jed, Schatz, Pat, Av, Emily and Pat, for not rolling their eyes, at least when I was there. Most of all, to my wife, Teresa, whose belief, support and inspiration has, from day one, never waned.

"Hell hath no fury like a woman scorned."

# <u>Chapter One</u>

**It had been a** little over two months since Dillon first arrived in Dublin, and things finally seemed to be settling down. He'd been living in the same unit for almost six weeks and no one had tried to kill him. Lucifer, the black mutt he'd found tied to his door with an anonymous note describing him as impossible, was still with him. He continued to work with the Irish cops, the Garda Síochána, and they hadn't threatened to deport him, at least lately. Abbey, his former neighbor with the long-stemmed roses tattooed on her lower back, had run into him on the street a few weeks back and was becoming an occasional friend with benefits.

He had his own vehicle, okay, it was a 2007 Opel Corsa, with almost a hundred and eighty thousand miles on it, the steering wheel on the right side and a stick shift he had to grind with his left hand, but still, he was getting used to it and hadn't side-swiped anything in a good two weeks.

He'd begun to take in some cultural things as well, learned a little more about the city, if not the island.

He'd been to Trinity College, seen the Book of Kells, the vast library with over two hundred thousand books. He toured the GPO, the General Post Office, and Croke Park. He'd walked through Stephen's Green and spent an afternoon at the Guinness Brewery.

All well and good, but tonight was going to be special. Rather than spend another night in the pub, he had a guest coming over this afternoon, and he planned to wine and dine and, well...

"You sure you can't stay the night? You only just got here forty minutes ago. I was thinking I could cook you dinner or we could go up to the shops, there's a little place that does a great job." Dillon had taken both pillows, propped them up behind his back, and was in the process of watching Lin get dressed. At the moment she was on her hands and knees looking for her thong.

"What'd you do with it? I mean, you just tossed it onto the floor, didn't you?" She looked up at Dillon as he took a sip of wine from her glass. "Hey, that's mine."

"Were you going to drink it?"

"Well no, I'd like to, but I have to drive. We're just a little tougher with our laws over here than you are in the States."

"So, then it's really not a problem if I take a sip."

She shot him a look.

"Okay, okay, sorry."

"You know, you could get out of bed and help me find the fecking thing. God, I just don't...."

"I would, but I'm just a little exhausted at the moment. I might be experiencing some sort of relapse and...."

"You're not experiencing any sort of relapse. You might be experiencing my foot up your hole if you don't help me. Besides, I checked your pulse, it was doing just fine if I recall."

"When did you check...oh, yeah," he said, remembering.

"So? Are you going to get your arse out of bed and help me?" she asked, then sat back on her heels with a puzzled look on her face.

He climbed out of bed with the notion that he knew exactly where her thong was.

"Now where do you think you're going?" she said as he walked out of the room.

He walked down the hall toward the bathroom. Lucifer, his ill-trained dog, was curled up against the spare room door, chewing something purple. Dillon reached down, grabbed the item and quietly said, "Bad dog, but I get it." Lucifer looked up at him, then followed him back toward the bedroom, but had enough sense not to enter.

"Here, sorry, I guess Lucifer has a thing for you, too," he said, and handed her what remained of her thong.

She held what was left of the item in both hands, then pulled the waist band and stared. "I can't wear this. There's literally nothing to wear."

7

"You want a pair of boxers?"

She rolled her eyes, picked the bottoms of her hospital scrubs up from the floor and stepped into them. She slipped into her bra, hooked it from behind, then pulled the scrub top over her head. "God, you and your dog. He's just as bad as you."

"Sure I can't cook you some dinner and then you could stay for breakfast?"

"I'd love to," she said not sounding at all convincing. "But it's my three-day weekend. I've got a 10K first thing in the morning for breast cancer and then tickets to the Leinster Munster match tomorrow night. I need to rest up." She stood on her tiptoes, gave him what barely passed as a kiss on the cheek, then headed down the stairs.

"Bad dog," she said to Lucifer down on the first floor. "See you, thanks," she called, then closed the front door behind her and was gone.

Dillon watched her out the window as she climbed into her car. She sat behind the wheel, dialed her cellphone and seemed to launch into an animated conversation as she pulled away.

He had two steaks marinating downstairs in the kitchen, an unopened bottle of wine on the counter he'd purchased especially for the night, and new candles in Waterford holders. So much for a relaxing evening at home.

# Chapter Two

**Weston Airport is a** small, private airport located just outside of Dublin, in County Kildare. It sits in a tranquil, rural setting and consists of one small runway just large enough to handle smaller, private planes. It features a restaurant, a bar, and a decently sized hangar with a number of small, private planes parked on the grass outside. The airport closes down at 8:30 in the evening during the summer months.

It was a good half-hour before that when the small plane made its final approach. The plane glided along the runway for a bit, touched ground, skipped slightly just once, then cruised toward the end of the runway where it turned and headed toward the large hangar. As it neared the hangar a heavy, dark blue, Mercedes van drove around the corner of the building and slowly pulled in front of the hangar.

The vehicle was a cash-in-transit van designed to do exactly what the name suggested, move cash. It was square-built with heavy steel walls and solid tires, what would be called an armored van in the States. Small,

9

bullet proof windows were imbedded in the rear of the van. A warning was posted on the rear door alerting everyone to the fact that the cash contents were attached to dye packs in the event of a robbery.

Two armed, uniformed men sat and waited in the van. Neither one spoke, but then what was there to say? They'd both done this dozens of times. They watched as the small plane approached. It moved up to the hangar, then turned, pulled forward maybe twenty feet and a moment later shut down.

The cash-in-transit van pulled alongside the plane, and the uniformed individual in the passenger seat stepped out of the van. He was armed with an automatic weapon and wore a protective vest beneath his uniform.

The small side door on the plane opened, and someone handed what looked like a grey case out the door to him. He hurried to the rear of the van, opened the door and set the case inside. A slightly built gentleman climbed out of the plane carrying an identical case, followed him to the rear of the van, and handed the case to the uniformed man. He set the case inside the van, closed the doors and gave a final, cautious look around the area.

The slightly built man smiled, nodded, waved farewell and then hurried back to the small airplane. As soon as he closed the door the plane turned round, taxied to the end of the runway and a moment later was cleared for takeoff.

The men in the van watched through the windshield as the plane traveled down the runway, picked up speed, hopped twice before it launched in the air, and sixty seconds later disappeared into the clouds.

They waited a moment, then made a gradual U-turn and headed back across the mostly empty parking lot. They stopped at the far end of the parking lot for a vehicle with its bright lights on to pass so they could turn.

The driver of a vehicle in the back of the parking lot said, "All right, perfect, I can see you coming down the road."

"I don't know, do you think they'll even stop?" The woman approaching the parking lot asked.

"They already have. You're doing just fine, just fine," he said, working to keep his voice calm. She'd no business being involved, and yet here she was, which meant he had to keep her on the straight and narrow. Just a minute or two more and it would all be over, then good riddance to both her and the boyfriend.

# **Chapter Three**

He'd developed a taste for the stuff, Guinness. Based on it's history, Dillon viewed it more as a health drink than a beer. Up until recently it was offered as a daily ration to those in hospital, so there were bound to be health benefits to a pint, which led him to his current off-duty undertaking. Just now he was in the process of appraising another cultural icon of Ireland, the pub.

He was in the Palace Bar, the back room of the Palace, actually, seated with his back to the wall in an armed chair. He'd been thinking about Lin and her rather hasty departure this afternoon when he noticed the three women looking for a place to sit in the crowded room.

They were blondes, with thick hair, and from their appearance, he guessed sisters. He had a small table in front of him, with three empty stools alongside the table.

The women glanced at the stools, but didn't make a move toward them, which marked them as tourists. That and the fact that they all had shopping bags from Carroll's, the Irish souvenir shops that were scattered on just about every other corner throughout Dublin city center.

It was Thursday night and the room was jammed. Another crowd was drinking outside on the sidewalk, with more people coming in the door every minute. For the moment it looked like Dillon controlled the only three available seats in the place.

"You want to sit down?" he called and sort of gestured toward the available stools.

They looked at each other for a long moment, a look on each face suggesting there had to be something better, somewhere. Two Dub's stepped into the room, scanned the place, spotted the open stools and took a step toward them.

One of the women, she looked to be the oldest of the three, tossed her shopping bag a good ten feet. The bag landed on top of a stool, perfectly, slid across it and up against the table.

"Where were you guys?" Dillon said hoping to make it sound like he'd been waiting for them. They smiled, hurried over and sat down. The two Dubs sort of frowned, turned and retreated toward the crowded barroom.

"Is it okay if we sit here?" the woman who so expertly tossed the shopping bag asked as she sat down. She had an American accent.

"Not a problem. Everyone does it. I mean sits at tables with folks they don't know. You're from the States?"

"Wisconsin," they all chimed in.

It fit. Blonde hair, blue eyes, beautiful skin. "Whereabouts in Wisconsin?"

"Milwaukee. Ever hear of it?" one of them asked, then proceeded to not wait for an answer. "We're just a little north of Chicago. On Lake Michigan. It's one of our Great Lakes, Michigan is. Well, and it's a State too, of course not the one we live in." She wore black jeans, black Nike shoes and a sort of creamy-colored sweater. Her hair was pulled back in a bun and she sat up very straight, ramrod straight. Dillon pegged her in the late thirties, maybe forty, but no more than that, and probably a school teacher.

"Isn't it great? You invite us to sit down, and we give you a geography lesson for free." This from the woman next to the teacher. She half shrugged and wrinkled her nose when she talked. She looked the youngest of the three. She would have been the spacey one.

"Carol," said the teacher. "He probably has never heard of Milwaukee, doesn't know about the Great Lakes and…"

"And is now regretting that he made the offer to us to sit down in the first place. Thanks." The oldest of the three smiled and extended her hand. "I'm Chris. This is my sister Carol and my sister Cindy."

Dillon shook her hand, said, "Nice to meet you. I'm Jack."

Chris held his hand for a moment. Carol shrugged and wrinkled her nose. Cindy the school teacher flashed a cold smile and pulled her jacket a little tighter around her shoulders.

"How long are you here for?" he asked.

"Four days, then back to the States. Sort of a whirlwind tour. We saw all of Dublin today. Blarney Castle and then over to the Cliffs of Moher tomorrow. Westport, in County Mayo, where our family is from the next day."

"We're Irish." Carol shrugged and wrinkled her nose, again.

"Oh, I thought you were American."

All three of them looked surprised at the response.

"Americans always say they're Irish, but the truth is they're American. They don't speak Irish, aren't from this country, wouldn't know what the GAA is or who's the Taoiseach."

"Do all Irish people hold that sort of opinion of Americans?" the school teacher named Cindy asked, and pulled her jacket just a little tighter.

"I wouldn't know, I'm an American."

"American? From where?"

"I guess all over, but mostly the midwest. Most recently the East coast."

"New York I bet, everyone's crabby there," Carol, the youngest, said.

"I'll get our drinks," the school teacher said.

"White," said Chris.

"Red," said Carol and wrinkled her nose again. Dillon was beginning to think it might be some sort of an involuntary twitch. "Where's the ladies' room?" Carol asked. He pointed to a set of stairs leading down

15

to a lower level. "Back in a minute," she said and hurried away, unbuckling her belt at the top of the stairs. Cindy the school teacher was right behind her.

"Oh, God, give me strength." Chris, the only one left at the table, gave an exasperated sigh.

"Long day?" Dillon asked.

"Yes. I mean, no, they're really great, it's just that we're sisters. You know, plenty of lady drama. Someone doesn't like the food, or the noise or the fact that that there's no ice cubes in the glass of water. They remember something one of us said at Thanksgiving dinner three years ago. Or they remember some perceived slight from high school. Whatever. Like I said, sisters."

"Nice you could all travel together."

"Yeah, at the end of the day we're very lucky and we know it."

They chatted for a couple of minutes. Dillon caught Carol and Cindy out of the corner of his eye, coming back up the steps from the ladies' room a few minutes later. They headed for the bar. Their older sister shook her head. "I know Cindy. She's going to ask to see the wine list, and then she'll want to argue with the bartender about which wine tastes like plums or cherries."

"They're four deep at the bar, waving twenty-euro notes to get a pint. This might not be the best place or the best time. Besides, I don't think they have a wine list. Probably just the same five or six they'll recite off the top of their head. Pints and whiskeys are more the thing here."

"She'll try anyway," she said, shaking her head.

The sisters were back ten minutes later. Cindy set a glass of white wine down in front of her sister. "Lots of luck, God knows what it tastes like. They don't even have a wine list."

"Jack was just telling me it's more of a pint and whiskey place."

"They could do a lot of business if they had a decent wine list," Cindy said, took a sip from her glass and winced. "Oooh."

Dillon looked around the packed backroom. There wasn't an available stool in the place, and customers were standing and chatting in the few areas with enough room. The barroom was packed, literally four deep waving cash for a drink, and the four bartenders were filling pint glasses as fast as proper pouring allowed. A crowd of twenty or thirty stood out front on the sidewalk, drinking pints. The last thing the Palace needed was a fancy wine list.

He felt his phone vibrating in his pocket, pulled it out and looked at the screen. McCabe. Shit.

# Chapter Four

**"Excuse me, I have** to take this. Hello," he said, waited a moment, then said, "Hang on for just a moment, I'm moving to a quiet spot where I can hear you. Pardon me, ladies." Cindy, the school teacher, put a disgusted look on her face. He began to wedge his way through the crowd, heading for the front door. It took a couple of minutes, getting past a couple of over-served jerks who didn't think they should have to move, but he finally made it out the door and stepped into the cobblestone street. "McCabe, you still there?"

"Where in the bleeding hell are you?"

"Out in front of the Palace. I couldn't hear you inside, and the place is packed, took a couple of minutes to get out. What's up?"

"We could maybe use your expertise."

"You debating which pub pours a better pint?"

McCabe ignored Dillon's attempt at humor. "Someone hit a cash-in-transit van. We've got two wounded. Apparently the shooter was American, or sounded American. I'm remembering your involvement with your man who robbed the armored car in New Jersey."

"Eddie Fleming? Yeah, but he's serving ten years in..."

"He's out."

"What do mean he's out? He was just..."

"Escaped, maybe six weeks ago. We apparently received an alert he was headed over here. One of our geniuses in the security office decided it would make more sense to sit on the information."

"Where are you now?"

"You're going to love it, Weston Airport."

"Not Dublin?"

"It's a small private airfield. Can you get to your car?"

"It's just a couple blocks away."

"Get onto the M4. Weston is in Leixlip, County Kildare. Take exit 5 on the M4, get onto the R403. See you in thirty minutes," he said and disconnected.

Dillon gave a longing look back toward the front door of the Palace. The three American women could argue about the wisdom of a wine list, who stole their boyfriends in high school, and why there wasn't any ice in the glass of water one of them would undoubtedly want. But they'd be doing it by themselves, without the grace and charm he always brought to the table. He took off at a trot toward his car.

He'd parked a good two blocks away, but knew he was lucky to even find a parking place he could squeeze into. Dublin wasn't exactly known for its parking options, and the few ramps they did have cost an arm and a leg, if you were lucky enough to even find a space once you got into a ramp.

Mercifully his car wasn't clamped and it hadn't been broken into. The Corsa sputtered to life on the second try, and he spent the next fifteen minutes getting out of the city center and making his way to the M4, a version of the interstate in the US, complete with bumper-to-bumper traffic jams during morning and afternoon rush hours.

# Chapter Five

**It was closer to** forty-five minutes before Dillon took the exit off the M4. He almost missed the sign shortly after that directing him onto the R403 road. "Road" was a generous term, it qualified only because there was pavement. With nothing resembling anything like a shoulder, and barely wider than a driveway, the road had impenetrable hedges and stone walls on either side. It ran parallel to the M4 just on the far side of a line of trees.

In short order, Dillon could see what appeared to be a large metal building up ahead with small aircraft parked behind it. Mercifully, he didn't meet any oncoming traffic. A few minutes later he saw the turn for the airport parking lot and, just beyond that, three vehicles with flashing lights.

He turned into the parking lot and was immediately stopped by a uniformed Garda officer who held his hand up as Dillon's brakes groaned. Behind the officer were a number of police vehicles, spotlights and yellow tape that said "DO NOT CROSS" wrapped around an area. A dark blue armored van, illuminated by a number of spotlights, sat in the middle of the taped off area. The driver's door on the armored van appeared to be open, and two individuals dressed in a hazmat suits were carefully examining the door. The name "Slándáil Transit" was painted in bright yellow letters with a red shadow across the front and along the side of the van.

Dillon lowered his window.

"Sorry, sir, I'm afraid there's no admittance for the time being," the officer said, and smiled. It was a polite smile, and the words were nice, but the tone left one with the distinct impression you weren't going to get in.

Dillon flashed a quick smile, pulled his ID out of his pocket and handed it to the officer. "I received a call from Inspector McCabe no more than fifty minutes ago. He interrupted what could have been shaping up to be a very pleasant evening. My name's Jack Dillon."

The officer glanced at the ID, then handed it back to Dillon. "Sorry, sir, didn't recognize you at first, do now," he said, giving a quick glance at the Corsa and flashing a questioning look. "That sounds like Inspector McCabe, just when you think you've got it all set, he gives you a call," he said. "Best park off to the side over there. Rumor has it there was a delivery of hot tea somewhere out here, but I'll be damned if I've been able to see it."

"Tell you what, if I come across the tea you can have my cup. Thanks," Dillon said, then ground the Corsa into gear and parked over on the far side of a half-dozen vehicles. He took his time walking over toward the activity, looking around as he made his way across the parking lot.

The lot looked like it could hold sixty or seventy cars. There were only maybe a dozen in the lot just now. All but four appeared to be police vehicles. At the front of the parking lot stood a three-story, buff-colored stucco building with four, small, private planes parked in a neat rank off to one side. A pair of lights hung on the outside of the building, just over the door, and more or less illuminated the parking area. A large, white metal structure Dillon took to be the hangar was on the other side of the building. The two planes and a helicopter Dillon had spotted as he drove in sat in the asphalt lot just behind the metal building.

"Dillon, Jack, over here." He looked and saw McCabe motioning him over to a group standing just behind a couple of spotlights trained on the blue van. He had both hands wrapped around a steaming paper cup, tea, Dillon figured, and he recalled the comment from the officer when he'd first pulled in. "Thanks for coming," McCabe said as Dillon approached.

"Not a problem. Since I have the night off and was attempting to relax, chatting up three gorgeous women hanging on my every word, what could be better than a call from you telling me to get my ass back to work?"

"Tea?" McCabe said, indicating his cup, smiling.

"Actually, now that you mention it, I wouldn't mind a cup. There's a bit of chill in the air."

McCabe's smile immediately disappeared. "Really? Christ, don't tell me you've taken a liking to this stuff."

"Anything to piss you off."

23

"I knew it. Well, help yourself, there's a canister over there." He indicated a table beneath a tent top with a large metal container sitting on it. Two guys were huddled around the container, involved in what looked like a serious discussion. Dillon could see steam drifting from their paper cups.

"Be right back," he said as McCabe nodded, then turned and started to talk with someone who'd just walked over to him. Dillon grabbed a paper cup from the stack, filled it with tea, grabbed two packets of sugar, and walked over to the cop who'd stopped his car at the entrance.

"Here, give this a taste and see if it's good enough for me to drink," he said. "Got you some sugar here if you take it. I didn't see any milk over there." The officer's name tag read, "Reilly, T."

"Aww, Jesus, you didn't have to do that, but very much appreciated. I'm running on fumes right about now."

"I never touch the stuff," Dillon said. "It might harden my baby face, and I can't have that."

"No, sir, certainly not," he said, then raised his steaming paper cup, and sort of blew on it. "Sláinte."

"How long you been out here?"

"Me?" He took a sip, gave a slight grimace, then gasped and seemed to savor the tea for a moment. "We were just about to head in for the day, my partner and me. We got the call and were the first ones on scene. How long we been out here? God, feels like days at this point."

"Where's your partner?"

24

"See that slovenly-looking plonker up there at the far end of the parking lot?" he indicated a space between the hangar and the three-story stucco building. Dillon could just barely make out the shadow of an individual leaning against the corner of the building.

"Have you given a statement?"

"Yeah, we both did, but then they wanted to separate the two of us. I guess in case something else came into our heads, they didn't want us comparing notes. We've got to do a *brief* follow-up interview before they'll let us go." His inflection on the word "brief" suggested anything but.

"Can you tell me anything?"

"I can tell you exactly what I told the last three people who asked me. We were just about to head back to the station at the end of our shift when the call came through. We responded to the call. I'm guessing it took maybe six or seven minutes to get here. The cash-in-transit van was right where you see it now. Your man in the passenger seat was slumped over. If he was breathing, it was just barely, and there was blood. A hell of a lot of blood. The driver was wounded, half hanging out of the door, half on the pavement, lying there on his back. We called for backup, pulled the guy out of the passenger seat and attempted some first aid, although I'm not sure how successful we were. There was just so much blood, an awful lot." His eyes had taken on a far-away look. He wasn't talking to Dillon now, he was back at the scene, trying to save some poor bastard he'd probably never met before.

He sort of blinked and came back to the here and now. "We didn't see anyone else. We never talked to whoever called it in initially. We just pulled the two of them out of the van, laid both of them on the pavement, tried to keep them alive, and waited."

"They say anything to you?"

"Your one from the passenger seat, he never regained consciousness, might have been dead for all we know, unresponsive, and of course all the blood. God, there was a lot of the stuff. The driver, he said something about a woman, said she *surprised* them or something, but mostly he was telling us to not let his partner die."

"A woman surprised them? What? Did he say what she did? She jumped out of the bushes or something?"

"No idea. We told him to just be quiet. Told him to relax, he was going to be okay, help was on the way, that sort of thing. Then he said 'American' a couple of times before he finally settled down."

"American? Like what? The woman was an American? There was an American with her? What did he mean?"

"He never got around to telling us. Poor soul had a lot of blood on him, too, an awful lot, but he kept telling us he was okay and to mind his partner."

"You notice anything about the van that…"

"Tell you the truth, sir, those are the same questions they asked me when I made my initial statement. Honestly, we were pretty damn busy, we had two wounded individuals who we thought needed care, a lot of care, and we were afraid some bastard might jump out of the bushes at just about any minute. In case you hadn't noticed, this isn't the States, we're unarmed."

Dillon nodded. The officer was right. Dillon planned to check the statements from him and his partner tomorrow. There was still plenty to learn. "Thanks. Good job, by the way. I don't know how badly these guys were wounded, but they've got a hell of a lot better chance because you and your partner were here first."

The cop smiled at that last bit, took a sip of tea and grimaced. "Mmm-mmm, not the best, but better than the one I didn't have. Thanks."

# Chapter Six

**Dillon headed back toward** the spotlights. There were a half-dozen of them lighting up the large, blue cash-in-transit van. Three guys were standing around, talking to, or rather, listening to, McCabe. "… stupid bollocks sat on the information and this is the result. What did you learn?" he asked, turning toward Dillon just as he drifted into the group.

"I'm guessing nothing you don't already know. They arrived on the scene, first responders, and found two people wounded. They were busy dealing with that, hoping to God whoever did the shooting didn't get a wild hair up their backside and decide to come back."

"He mention the driver talking?"

"Yeah. What he said was the guy told them something about a woman and an American, or did he mean an American woman? Or hell, for that matter did he mean an American car? Hard to tell at this point. Said the driver was bloody, but wanted them to help his partner."

"We'll send someone to the hospital," McCabe said. "We'll be denied access for the moment. Initial reports are the wounds on one of them aren't life-threatening, I'm guessing that's the driver. I'm presuming the other lad is still in surgery, which doesn't sound all that positive."

"Any time you're shot it's serious. Back up for a moment, did you say 'wounds'? Plural?"

"I did. Three as far as we know. A bit sketchy yet, but initial reports say right arm, right shoulder and a graze on the head. I'm guessing that's what probably saved him. He maybe looked dead, maybe he was unconscious or something. His partner took a round in the side or the chest, not sure which exactly. You have any idea how this shapes up with what you know of your man Fleming and the way he's operated in the past?"

"Eddie Fleming, that bastard. He's been armed, he's fired a weapon, to my knowledge he's never been involved with anyone being shot. That doesn't mean he's not capable, just that it hasn't happened. Yet."

"His specialty was cash-in-transit vans?"

"'Armored vans,' we say. Yeah, his initial robberies were vans, or actually the team on the van as they were restocking ATMs. You can see a definite pattern of sophistication over a period of about thirty-six months. Like I said, he started out robbing the team restocking the ATM. Then he upped his game and hit a van en route to a number of ATMs. After that he hit the supposedly secure facility where the vans were stocked, and then his last brain fart, an attempted hit on the

Federal Reserve in Minneapolis. That's where it all went bad."

"Finally got the bastard," one of the guys said. He looked familiar, in fact they all did, sort of, but Dillon couldn't place any names. McCabe was the only one he knew, and he certainly didn't know McCabe all that well.

"The thing with Eddie Fleming is, he became rather adept at learning the inner workings of the industry. He somehow got access to the schedules of when and where the various local restockings were going to take place. Then he gained access to when the vans themselves were going to be stocked. And then, finally, he knew when the Federal Reserve branch was going to be moving a large amount of cash. He basically worked his way up the banking food chain, and to this day no one can figure out how he managed to do that. He may be a bastard, I'll give you that much, but he sure as hell isn't stupid."

"Considering the shootings tonight," Dillon continued, "Fleming's been armed in the past, but to actually be involved in shooting someone? To the best of my knowledge this would be a first. I know you had a rumor he was going to attempt to come over here, but from that to actually tying him into this is a bit of a stretch at this juncture."

"The other question is why here? Maybe the bar has an ATM, but someone on Fleming's level would almost be too embarrassed to stoop that low. What could it be stocked with? A grand? Two at the most? It wouldn't be worth the risk. I can't see him being that desperate."

"I think we're about to find out," someone said, then indicated a car stopped by the Garda at the entrance to the parking lot. As they all sort of turned and looked, the officer nodded to whoever was in the dark-colored car and pointed in the group's general direction. A moment later the car headed toward the van and the group.

# __Chapter Seven__

__They watched as a__ Mercedes slowly approached
and parked maybe fifteen feet from them. It was dark
blue, almost the same color as the van, only a lot
sleeker-looking. Dillon couldn't tell what the particular
model was, but suffice it to say the vehicle was
probably out of his price range, expensive, very
expensive.

Dillon found it interesting that all of them had
parked in marked spaces in the parking lot. Even though
it was after hours and they were here investigating a
crime, virtually all of them, by force of habit, had
parked between the lines painted on the asphalt, even
McCabe, who was notorious for pulling into a no-
parking zone.

The Mercedes, apparently, didn't feel the need. Not
only did it not feel the need to comply, it actually
parked in the lane designated for exiting traffic,
essentially parking against the traffic flow. Not that it
really made a difference, the place was closed, virtually

empty, and it would hardly be an inconvenience to just pull around the car. But still.

The passenger door opened up and a man climbed out of the car. Dillon guessed him at maybe six feet, and from the distance he looked in reasonable shape. He was dressed in a grey suit that appeared to have some sort of sheen to it. He wore a black t-shirt beneath the suit coat with a black pocket square in the breast pocket. He had dark, curly hair on top with sides that appeared to be shorn with a razor. Dillon pegged his age at maybe early forties. He stood alongside the Mercedes, and tugged at the hem of his coat, waiting while the driver walked around the front of the car. The driver looked to be ten to fifteen years older, maybe mid-fifties. He wore a dark, pinstripe suit with a white shirt and striped tie.

"Oh shit," someone whispered behind Dillon.

"Inspector McCabe," the younger man called out making a beeline for McCabe. "Eamon Dunne," the man called, seeming to pick up his pace and attack with an outstretched hand. As he shook hands with McCabe he half turned. "I'm sure you remember my solicitor, Tully McBride."

"Guilty as charged, the pair of them," the voice behind Dillon said, only this time a good bit quieter.

McCabe nodded "hello," but his body language suggested he wasn't all that pleased to see the two of them here. There was a momentary pause, a bit too long, like the two newcomers were waiting for some sort of earth-shattering statement that just was not going to happen.

"So what have you got for us?" Dunne finally asked.

"Nothing, actually. I'm sure you must understand, as you can see we're just getting underway in what, by all initial indications, will be an ongoing investigation covering all facets."

"But surely you must have some idea what occurred, who's responsible and where they're off to. Even the Garda can't be that obtuse. Now, what, exactly, can we do to help?"

"For Christ sake," someone muttered off to the side.

"What can you do?" McCabe said. "Well for starters, Simmons," McCabe called.

The voice behind Dillon groaned, "Fuck."

"Simmons, if you'd be so kind as to take a statement from Mr. Dunne. We'll need everything regarding the van. Names of the driver and passenger. Their purpose for being here. Activity prior to arriving here and any planned activity following. Home addresses, spouses, church…"

"That's the stuff, give it to 'em, boss," someone whispered, and another voice snickered.

"Gentlemen, if you'd care to join me over here," Simmons said, heading toward the tent with the canister of tea and not waiting for a reply. Dunne seemed about to say something to McCabe, but McBride, the solicitor, took hold of his arm and somewhat forcibly pulled him in the opposite direction, following Simmons.

"Plonker," the guy next to Dillon growled as they watched the three of them head toward the tea canister.

"What'd I miss?" Dillon asked.

"Eamon Dunne, he's one of the in crowd. Does all his business on the back of an envelope in a parking lot at midnight. We've been investigating him for a good few years. Always able to worm his way out, but we'll get the bastard sooner or later. A tad too many coincidences over the years."

"A right cute hoor," another said.

"So what's his connection to this?"

He scoffed and shook his head. "Wouldn't you know, the bastard owns the cash-in-transit company."

"You're kidding?"

"I wish."

# **Chapter Eight**

**After a few more** hours they had a handful of basic facts. The van appeared to have been struck on the front left side by another vehicle, possibly grey in color. A forensic team had gathered paint chip samples and measured a skid mark on the pavement. Skid marks at the rear of the van suggested a second vehicle. It was suspected of traveling at a higher rate of speed than normal for the area, had screeched to a stop, leaving skid marks approximately five feet in length. It did not appear that the van had been hit from the rear, but the assumption was that with the two vehicles, one in front and one in the rear, the van had effectively been blocked in place.

"Thoughts?" McCabe asked. There were six of them standing in the parking lot. By now it was a little after three in the morning. A heavy-duty tow truck was in the process of winching the cash-in-transit van up onto its bed to be hauled away for further examination.

Everyone in the group looked tired.

Simmons, the guy who'd taken the statement from Eamon Dunne spoke first. "The reason the cash-in-transit was on site has nothing to do with the ATM in the restaurant. They were at the airport tonight because they receive periodic currency deliveries here. And that's what they were doing tonight, receiving a delivery of currency. They were in contact with the plane and waiting at the airport before the plane arrived, which is standard operating procedure."

"If everything goes as planned the transfer of cash shouldn't take more than four or five minutes from the time the plane touches down until it's cleared for takeoff once the transfer has been made. By all indications that's exactly the way things happened this time around."

"Your man Eamon Dunne was probably just waiting in the weeds for the plane to leave before he attacked two of his employees," someone said. A couple of heads nodded in agreement.

"Well, if that's the case, then he attacked his younger brother, because he was one of the men in the van. Not sure which one he was, both men in the van were wounded. Mr. Dunne did not appear to be too happy with that news."

"Bastard would gladly sell his own mother if he could find someone to take the bitch."

"What about access to knowledge about this?" someone asked.

"How much are we talking?" another said.

"Delivery was two-point-five million euros," Simmons said, then just let that number sort of hang out there for a long moment while it sank in. "As to who knew? Officially, it was limited to Eamon Dunne."

"There you go," a voice said.

"I knew it," someone from the back of the group half-shouted.

Simmons gave a look in reply, then said, "I know our dealings with Mr. Dunne and some of his undertakings over the years have not been the best. But let me go out on a limb and suggest this may different. His younger brother Paddy was wounded, he might be the one seriously wounded and, the company stands to lose a good deal of money here."

Someone in the back started to comment, and Simmons quieted them with quick wave of his hand.

"Now hold on just a minute. This is insured, no doubt, but if the funds aren't recovered, Dunne's rates will go through the bleeding roof and at some point he'll end up having paid at least that much back to the insurance company for coverage, maybe more. Okay? So you've got your man's brother shot, and you've got his insurance rates rising to the level where they just might put him out of business. Those are two factors we have to consider."

"Now, here's the third thing. They receive two to three deliveries like this a week, every week, right here at this airport. A crew from Slándáil Transit drives out here three times a day, morning, noon and night, every day, seven days a week. Most of those times nothing happens, there's no delivery. So what that might mean is that someone had information, in advance, that this *'delivery'* was the real deal. It would seem the logical

38

question would be who had the information? Dunne obviously knew. Did anyone else? And if so, who are they?"

It was quiet for a long moment, then McCabe scanned the crowd and sighted in on Dillon.

*Oh shit, please don't,* thought Dillon.

"Marshal Dillon, your thoughts please on this American, Eddie Fleming."

# <u>Chapter Nine</u>

**Dillon had never heard** of, let alone met, Eddie Fleming until after Fleming been arrested, charged and convicted for attempting to steal close to four million dollars from the Minneapolis Federal Reserve. That was back in 2014. The *meeting* consisted of Dillon transporting him back to New Jersey on a two-and-a-half-hour Delta flight to LaGuardia airport. Aside from the fact that the US Marshal's Service was going to deliver him to a New Jersey prison where he was going to serve four years, and then, after serving, deliver him back to Minneapolis to serve a twelve-year stint, he came across as a nice enough guy, if you liked career criminals.

"My thoughts on Eddie Fleming. He's not stupid. He got caught in the States attempting to knock off an armored van transporting cash from the Minneapolis Federal Reserve to a bank headquarters. It was merely happenstance that they caught him. As most, if not all, of you know, he escaped from a US prison about six weeks ago. I don't have any details on that right now, I only found out about it tonight, but as soon as I get the details I'll pass them on."

"That said, if he was involved here, it is, to my knowledge, the first time anyone has been injured during one of his robbery attempts. I don't believe he has ever shot anyone prior to tonight, and we don't know if he was even involved, nor if in fact, he did the shooting. On the other hand, it may represent a graduation to a more violent tactic in the course of committing a crime. I honestly don't know. I can suggest that if he finds this method successful, look for some fine-tuning and then it will occur again. Once he lands on something that works, he plays it for all he can get."

It was quiet for a moment. Fatigue had set in. McCabe broke the silence. "I'd like Marshal Dillon and Simmons to stay. The rest of you head home and get some sleep. We'll hit the ground running in the daylight. Goodnight."

McCabe and Simmons watched as people headed toward their cars. As the first of the cars started up and began to head back toward Dublin city, McCabe said, "I want the two of you to head over to the hospital and wait there until you can talk to one or both of the victims. We need information, any information."

"Which hospital are they at, Inspector?" Simmons asked.

"Hospital? Oh, yes, of course. Sorry about that. They've been taken to Blanchardstown, James Connolly Hospital. You've been there before, haven't you, Simmons?"

"More times than I care to remember, sir." Simmons turned toward Dillon and said, "I'm guessing you don't know the way, so you can follow me." They both said their goodbyes to McCabe and headed to their cars, Dillon thinking he'd kill for a couple hours of sleep in his own bed right about now.

It was still dark outside. At least the traffic wasn't bad. Some time later Dillon checked his watch and realized it had taken less than thirty minutes before they pulled in front of the James Connolly Hospital.

Simmons was driving an official vehicle with Garda markings all over it and flashing lights on the top. Dillon pulled his Corsa up close in the no-parking zone behind Simmons and turned the car off. Simmons was out of his car before the Corsa had finished sputtering, and hurried back to Dillon carrying what looked like a sheet of white cardboard.

"Here, set this on the dash so some plonker doesn't ticket or clamp you for parking there," he said, handing Dillon an official-looking sign that read, "An Garda Síochána" with a very official-looking gold crest before and after the words. "Hopefully, they'll still be in recovery and we'll be able to grab some sleep in one of the waiting rooms or in a hallway."

The information counter had a sign sitting on it that read "Closed," but Simmons seemed to know where he was going. They walked around a corner and took the elevator up to the third floor, then walked through a maze of halls before finally ending up at a nurses station. Two nurses, a redhead and a brunette sat at a desk, working their way through a stack of files. Both nurses wore blue hospital scrubs, and for a brief moment Dillon thought of Lin stopping over after her shift.

"Good morning, ladies," Simmons said.

Both women looked up. The redhead yawned. The brunette said, "Good God, if it ain't Detective Simmons. I should have known you'd be up here sooner or later. Sorry about your news."

"You mean the shootings?" Simmons said.

"Well yes, of course that, but your man, you know, him not making it out of the operating room."

"Not making it? Actually no, this is the first I, that we've heard of it." Both women looked at Dillon. "Oh, forgive me, this is Marshal Dillon. He's American," Simmons said, adding the last part and making it sound like Dillon had some sort of communicable disease.

"Marshal?" the redhead said.

"My name's Jack. Nice to meet you, Mary and Anne," Dillon said, reading their nametags.

"Nice to meet you, Marshal Jack. Are you a cowboy, then?" Mary, the redhead, asked. She sounded serious.

"No, just a Marshal."

"You said one of them passed?" Simmons asked.

"Yes, Mr. Dunne."

"Paddy Dunne?" Simmons asked, as if there had been more than one man named "Dunne" in the cash-in-transit van.

"Yes, that's the one. The other, Thomas O'Brien, is in recovery, room 305," Ann the brunette said. She ran her fingers across the keyboard in front of her, glanced at the screen and said, "No complications. We have him sedated just now."

Simmons looked at Dillon. "I better give McCabe a call. Losing Paddy Dunne isn't going to help matters and is liable to add some complications. If you'll pardon us, ladies." Mary, the redhead, gave another big yawn, and then they both went back to working on the stack of files.

Simmons indicated the end of the hallway with a nod of his head, and Dillon followed after him. There was a double window with a view that looked out onto an area with four dumpsters. It was still dark enough outside that a street light illuminated the area around the dumpsters. A parking lot, empty at this hour except for two or three cars, extended beyond the dumpsters.

Off-white vinyl couches that looked like a cheap version of a retro-Scandinavian style were pushed up against either side of the hall. A white, Formica-topped coffee table sat between the two couches. The table was too large for the area, and forced one to step sideways to take a seat on one of the couches. A corner of the Formica-top table had been chipped off at a jagged angle, and looked like someone had taken a large bite out of the table. At least four squiggly brown stains from cigarettes snaked their way across the Formica. Tea cups and three dog-eared fashion magazines were scattered across the top of the table. A headline in bright-blue, "Kardashian Krazy," screamed across one of the covers, which pretty much eliminated Dillon from the mix of potential readers.

"Might as well grab a seat and try to get some sleep," Simmons said. Rather than wiggle in between the couch and the coffee table, he took a seat on the wooden arm of the couch. He placed his cellphone up to his ear, glanced at Dillon and then waited a moment. Dillon cleared the paper tea cups from the table, then stretched out with his feet resting across the far end of the table.

"Yes, Inspector, sorry to bother you," Simmons said, and shot a look at Dillon. "No sir, sedated. Some bad news, I'm afraid. We just heard from the nurses, your man, Paddy Dunne, apparently didn't make it. I don't know that, sir. Yes, I'm presuming they'll notify next of kin if they haven't already. We will, sir. Not a bother, comfy as can be in the waiting area," Simmons said and rolled his eyes. "Very good, sir. Yes, just as soon as we're able. Yes, I'm looking at him, now, sir," Simmons said, and nodded toward Dillon. "Thank you. You, too, sir."

"Everything okay?" Dillon asked. He was moving back and forth across a corner of the vinyl couch, attempting to find a comfortable alternative to his current position and failing miserably.

"He wants us to stay here, at least for the time being. Hopefully at some point we'll be able to talk to Tommy O'Brien. I'm going to get the recording equipment out of the car and be back in a minute. I don't want to be chasing after it once we get the word O'Brien is available. You might as well try and get some sleep, if he's sedated it could well be noon before we're able to talk with him."

45

Simmons walked back down the hall, and Dillon attempted to find a more comfortable position. A few moments later he heard laughter coming from the direction of the nurses station, turned, and saw Simmons involved in the telling of some joke. He settled back into the couch and gradually drifted off to a fitful sleep. Simmons woke him briefly as he jarred the coffee table while trying to quietly lie down on the other couch. Someone began polishing the hallway floor not three feet from where they were trying to sleep twenty minutes after that. Sometime after the floors were polished, a cart stacked with clanging breakfast trays was wheeled next to the room closest to the couches. A truck backed up outside, with its back-up warning alarm sounding. It picked up all four dumpsters one by one, and emptied them into a large bin. The crushing mechanism on the truck was then activated to make room for the next dumpster's contents, which meant that the truck had to pull ahead and then back up with the alarm sounding once again.

It all made for a fitful few hours.

# __Chapter Ten__

**Dillon didn't think he'd** fallen asleep, but the next thing he knew, someone was shaking his shoulder. As he opened his eyes he thought he heard a truck groaning outside, and his first thought was the idiot who'd emptied the dumpsters had returned. It turned out to be Simmons, snoring. He looked into the face of a nurse with brunette hair. Not the woman he'd met a few hours earlier.

"Mr. O'Brien is awake and about to have breakfast. You can see him if you'd like, but only for a minute or two."

Dillon sort of stretched and groaned. "What time is it?"

She seemed to recoil for a moment, then said, "It's almost ten. I'll leave you the pleasure of waking Simmons over there," she said, just as Simmons gave a loud snore in response.

Dillon sat up, rubbed his eyes and attempted to get his bearings. As he turned his head from side to side, he could feel his neck crack, and heard an audible snap, crackle and pop. He rolled his shoulders and got a similar effect.

The sun was up and shining outside on what appeared to be a beautiful morning. He stood up from the torturous couch, and heard his knees and lower back crack. He left Simmons to sleep for another five minutes and set off to find the restroom. He planned to ask directions at the nurses station.

The nurse who woke him just a minute earlier watched as he approached. Just as Dillon was about to open his mouth she said, "Down the hall, take the first right, then take the next left and it's on the left-hand side. You'll find it just after the door marked 'maintenance.'" She followed up with an insincere smile.

"Thank you."

"Oh, you're the American?"

"Yes."

"These can't hurt," she said, placing two red and white peppermints on the counter in front of him and flashing another insincere smile.

"Gee, thanks."

He found the mens room, studied himself in the mirror for a long moment and decided that all things considered he really didn't look that bad. Suddenly the door swung open and Simmons stepped in.

"You look like absolute shite," he said by way of greeting.

"Good morning, my precious," Dillon replied. "You get the word? O'Brien is up and eating breakfast. That battle-ax nurse said we could only have a couple of minutes with him. Told me it was 'doctor's orders.'"

"They always tell you a couple of minutes. That's Grania, the nurse. Actually, she's okay, she runs a tight ship. Once you let her know you understand she's in charge, you'll be her best friend."

"She gave me a couple of mints, like I had bad breath or something. God, I barely even spoke to her."

"They look like these?" Simmons asked and pulled two of the red and white peppermints from his pocket. "They can't hurt. Wouldn't want your man O'Brien passing out on us now, would you?"

He unwrapped one of the peppermints and tossed it into his mouth. Dillon followed suit and did the same. "Let's go have our chat with Mr. Thomas O'Brien, see what we can learn before the Queen Bee, Nurse Grania, tosses us out."

# Chapter Eleven

**Dillon followed Simmons to** room 305. They stopped at the door and Simmons whispered, "Let's not make any mention of Paddy Dunne. I don't want your man any more upset than he already is."

He quietly knocked on the door, pushing it open as he knocked. His knock was soft enough that Tommy O'Brien didn't answer. Then again, maybe O'Brien chose to ignore the two of them, or maybe his hearing had been affected by the shots fired at such close range.

The hospital room was small by American standards, consisting of just two beds, a bathroom and two plastic visitor's chairs. Thankfully, the second bed was unoccupied. A white curtain was draped around O'Brien's bed and, at the moment, partially pulled back. A television, mounted on the wall opposite his bed, was playing although the sound was off. It looked like some sort of woman's fashion show was on at the moment. Three women were standing on the set with the camera focused on their shoes.

"Mr. O'Brien," Simmons called as he entered, and O'Brien looked up from the remnants of his breakfast. All things considered, after being shot three times less than twenty-four hours earlier, he looked in awfully good shape. He'd a black eye and a swollen, bruised cheek. The left side of his upper lip was swollen slightly and the skin was split across the bridge of his nose. But his nose didn't appear to be broken, and you had to stare for a moment before you realized his upper lip was swollen. He had a gauze bandage wrapped around his head, some bandaging on his left shoulder, and his left arm was in a sling. He'd been eating a strip of bacon, holding it in his right hand when they'd entered, and he now tossed the bacon back onto his plate. He picked up a paper napkin with his right hand and sort of rubbed it between his fingers as he looked at the two of them.

*Probably thinks were doctors,* Dillon thought.

"Hi."

"We're Garda Síochána," Simmons said, flipping out a black leather case that held his badge and ID. He waited a brief moment to ensure the point had been made before snapping the case closed. "This is Marshal Dillon. He's with the American Marshals Service. He's been assigned to us to help work this case."

O'Brien nodded, looked suitably impressed, studied Dillon for a moment, then said, "Whatever helps you catch these bastards."

"Mind if I call you Tommy?" Simmons asked.

O'Brien shook his head no and said, "Everyone does."

"Thanks, Tommy. We just want to ask you a couple of questions. See if you can't add to what we already know and help us nail the bastards that did this to you. How you feeling, by the way?"

"Pretty good, I guess, under the circumstances. Don't mind telling yas they scared the shite out of me."

Simmons nodded. They were becoming fast friends. "Well, you're an awfully lucky man. It could have been a lot worse."

"How's Paddy doing? He's my partner. I couldn't get an answer from any of the nurses I asked."

Simmons didn't even blink. "I think they have him in recovery after the surgery, we've been told he's sedated. Afraid that's about all we know at this point. Say, I'd like to record our conversation if that's okay? It'll save us some time, not having to explain things over and over to folks, you know. And I want to make sure we don't miss anything you tell us."

"Yeah, sure, not a problem."

Simmons slid the breakfast tray over, and said, "Jack, maybe set this on the window sill so it's not in the way. We got this old recorder, thing looks a sight, but she works. You want to hang onto that plate, Tommy? Those strips of bacon look awfully good. Be a shame to let 'em go cold."

He seemed to think about that for half a second, then said, "You sure it's okay? I mean, if it's a problem…."

"Not a problem," Simmons said, then he picked up the plate and nodded at Dillon to take the tray away.

Dillon walked the tray over to the window sill, noticed that the sunny sky from fifteen or twenty minutes earlier was now completely grey. A spattering of misty rain coated the window. Typical, you don't like the Dublin weather just wait fifteen minutes and it was bound to change.

"Help yourself," Simmons said, setting the plate back down on the tray table. Tommy grabbed a piece of bacon with his right hand, took a bite, started chewing and smiled.

Simmons placed an antique, black tape recorder on the tray table. The thing was held together with two pieces of duct tape on one end and a worn, paint-splattered, black leather case on the other. He pushed a button, and a window opened in the center of the recorder. He inserted a cassette tape.

Dillon didn't know you could even get cassette tapes anymore, let alone a blank one. And just where could you find a cassette recorder that actually worked?

"Bit of ancient history here, Tommy," Simmons said, then did a test counting to five, replayed it to make sure it was audible, and then started the tape rolling. He gave the time, the date and their location, introduced them one by one, and then nodded at Tommy O'Brien.

"So, in your own words, Tommy, can you tell us what happened?"

"Honestly, not an awful lot to tell. We were working the evening shift. Anyone who works it goes out to the airport at around seven-forty-five. We all do it, every day of the week. Sometimes we pick up a delivery, sometimes no delivery comes in. We wait out there until

53

half past eight, then we go back to the office and punch out for the day. If you pick up a delivery we're maybe in the office twenty minutes earlier. Rain or shine, we're out there."

"And what was the situation last night?"

"We picked up the delivery. See, they actually radio the office and whoever is at the airport, a simultaneous thing, letting both parties know at the same time. In the case of last night, it was Paddy and me out at the airport. Nothing out of the ordinary. We'd been waiting out there for maybe ten or fifteen minutes. We picked up two boxes, Paddy set them in the van, then just like always we waited until the plane took off. I just described no more than six or seven minutes that the plane was on the ground. We watched them take off, like we're supposed to do, and then we headed back to the office."

"Like any other time we drove across the parking lot, last night we had to wait for a car to pass. It was coming at us with its bright lights on, no indicator to signal a turn, and then just when it's about to pass the fool turns sharp and clips us."

"Damage to the car?"

"Probably some, had to be more than whatever happened to our van. I mean the thing's built like a tank, literally. So, next thing I know, this sort of little old lady jumps out, hurries over to my door, she's apologizing and everything, talking a mile a minute. Asking, were we all right? Saying she's sorry. We were kind of thinking it was funny, and then the next thing I know the bitch suddenly shoves this pistol in my face. I

54

hear a noise behind us, look in the side view mirror, and another car had just skidded to a stop to block us in. I could have probably driven over either vehicle, pushed 'em the hell out of the way, but your woman had that gun in my face. Paddy went for his weapon and then all hell broke loose. Bitch shot him, I kicked my door open to knock her on her ass, but she just sort of jumped back and then shot me, too."

"I think I tried to tell the Garda when they first arrived, but to be honest, I was probably in shock. I'm not sure what the hell I said to them except I wanted them to take care of Paddy. He wasn't looking all that good."

"Can you give us a description of the woman?"

"The woman?"

"You said she was a little old lady."

"That's what I thought, at least at first. Sort of grey hair, some silly kind of hat. Dark dress of some kind. I mean, she looked old, not what you'd call attractive, if you know what I mean. The bitch went on jabbering, asking were we all right, and saying she was sorry. I remember thinking, would you just shut the hell up. Paddy and me, we kinda smiled at each other. Then, the next thing I hear is this skid behind us, sort of see this car, but it was getting dark and the bastard didn't have any lights on."

"Then, I remember looking at this old wan and thinking, you ain't an old woman, maybe you're a wanker, and suddenly all hell breaks loose and she's shooting us. I mean, it took a bit of time to tell you all

55

this, but I'd say it all happened in just five, maybe ten seconds. Really fast. Honest."

"What made you think she might be a man?"

"She was talking in this crazy girly sort of voice, kinda squeaky and a real pain in the arse to hear. At first I'm thinking she's some crazy one, but the more I'm hearing it in my head the more I think she was trying to pull the blinders on us. Then I'm pretty sure she'd a wig on, 'cause it sort of slipped down a bit on her forehead. I remember her pushing it back up, me thinking she was a real wacko, and then the next thing I know she just started shooting."

"She have any sort of accent, out the west, maybe from the north or maybe sounding like a Dub?"

"Yeah, pretty sure it was American, well, maybe. I got cousins over there in the States, Ohio. She sounded sort of like them. I kinda, sorta think she was American, but I can't be sure, oh, and she had a nice set on her," he said, almost sounding like he was bragging.

"American, anything special she said that makes you think that?"

"Yeah, the way she talked, I mean the words, you know how they are. She said 'blinker' instead of 'indicator.'"

"What?"

"You know, when you turn. She said she had her blinker on, that's what the Yanks say, not 'indicator'. That old bitch said 'blinker.'"

The door opened and Nurse Grania stepped into the room. That was all she did, take a step in, and then stood there holding the door open. "Gentlemen, time is up. I'm about to administer another sedative to Mr. O'Brien. I'm sorry, but if he's going to recover it's a necessary evil." She seemed to take pleasure in that last bit, the "necessary evil" part.

"We're finished up, for the moment," Simmons said. He signed off on the recording, giving the time they concluded and stating medical reasons for the conclusion. "Tommy, you get better soon, and thank you. You've been a help, a very big help." Then he turned to Dillon and said, "You have any questions, Marshal?"

"Gentlemen," Nurse Grania said, a bit more insistent.

"How tall was this woman?"

"Tall? I don't know, about average, I'd guess. I mean, maybe a little tall for a woman, not quite up to your shoulder I'd say."

"You pick up on anything like a birthmark, hair color?"

"No, nothing comes to mind. Course, like I said, I'm thinking she was wearing a wig. I remember she had lipstick and I remember thinking she did a shitty job of putting it on. Oh and brown or green eyes, couldn't tell which, actually."

"Gentlemen, now I really must insist," Nurse Grania said.

Simmons pressed stop on his antique recorder. They said thanks once more and headed out the door.

# Chapter Twelve

**"Thoughts?" Simmons asked. They** were standing alongside their cars in front of the hospital, catching a long, dirty look from a woman pushing a stroller and heading for the front door. She glanced at the no-parking zone, then back at the two of them. The sidewalk was still damp from the misty rain, but the sky had more or less cleared and the sun was back.

"Yeah. First of all, clever move, signing off and leaving the recorder playing. Don't know how far that would go in court, but…"

"Depends on the type of crime. This show, I could go just about all the way now that someone was murdered. You pick up anything for him?"

"My first thought is he's awfully damn lucky not to be lying in some morgue next to Paddy Dunne. Three shots at close range and he's sitting up eating breakfast the following morning, I could use some luck like that."

"Couldn't we all."

"It could have been Eddie Fleming dressed as the woman. Of course, the height's wrong, Fleming's an even six feet, and the son of a bitch has blue eyes, bright blue eyes. It's all pretty sketchy. The diversion, a woman driving into the van, that could be Fleming. It's clever enough to be him, but it still leaves the big question."

"Which is?"

"How in the hell did they know about the cash delivery?"

"Yeah, I don't know about that. Under any other circumstances, I'd be ready to pounce on Eamon Dunne. I can guarantee you he'd be in right now getting the third degree. But with his brother getting killed, it just doesn't feel right. McCabe will have someone checking out the brothers' relationship, you can bet on that."

"Which reminds me. I want to put a call into the States, have someone check on Fleming's travels."

"You think he'd have a passport?"

"I think he probably traveled on a fake passport, but just in case I'd like to have my contact check with passport control here."

"I'm sure McCabe already has someone checking into it."

"Good, then my friend will just increase the pressure a bit. The wild card is still the shooting, that's not the Fleming I know. And from the way Tommy O'Brien talked, they were already held at gunpoint. Why would you try and reach for a gun? It would be like committing suicide."

"Maybe that's what it was."

Somehow Dillon didn't think so. They climbed into their respective vehicles. Simmons started up, seemed to check something for a moment, then pulled away.

Dillon's Corsa groaned in complaint before finally starting on the fourth try. He let the vehicle warm up for a moment, just long enough to catch the evil eye from two guys walking out the front door. They both focused on the Garda sign sitting on the dashboard. One of them shook his head and swore. Dillon pulled away from the curb and headed back to his place.

He was halfway home before he remembered Lucifer. His ill-trained, misbehaving, thong-chewing dog had been on his own since about eight o'clock last night. God only knew what sort of trouble he'd gotten into.

He met Dillon at the front door. As soon as he unlocked the door, Lucifer hurried out, ran about four feet, then turned to stare at Dillon as he squatted and proceeded to relieve himself. Based on the effort, he had clearly been waiting for some time. Dillon watched him as Lucifer finally stood, then kicked his back legs a few times in an effort to bury his deposit.

"Come on, Lucifer, let's go for a walk," he called, then stepped into the house. The dog dutifully followed. The kitchen wastebasket had been knocked over and the contents were scattered throughout the kitchen and the front entryway. To the right, in the sitting room, the right front leg on Dillon's new couch had been chewed down to half its original size. Bits and slivers of wooden couch leg were scattered about the room. Upstairs, he seemed to have been able to somehow grab hold of the toilet paper roll and unravel it, pulling it down the hall and into master bedroom. In the middle of the bedroom floor lay the remnants of a silky black thong. Dillon didn't have the foggiest idea who it might have belonged to.

He wanted to drop kick the little bastard out the window, but he couldn't really blame him. He re-rolled the toilet paper as best he could. Took what was left of the thong and tossed it into the kitchen wastebasket with the rest of the debris scattered throughout the first floor. He swept up the bits of wooden leg from his new couch, then vacuumed the rug. In the end he felt thankful Lucifer hadn't pooped in the house. He dutifully cleaned up the dog's recent deposit in the front garden, then grabbed his leash and took him for a short walk.

They walked over to Albert College Park, on Ballymun Road, just next to DCU. It was about one-point-two miles around the park, with beautifully cared-for grounds and plenty of dogs being walked, all of which Lucifer ignored, because after all, he was better than they were. They had made it just about to the furthest point from home when Dillon's cellphone rang.

"Dillon," he answered.

"Dildo, it's me, Sean." Sean Flynn, one of the guys from the squad. A good head. "McCabe would like the honor of your presence, if you can fit it into your busy schedule."

"Yeah, sure, where are you?"

"Actually, not too far from your place. Which is why I'm calling. You're home, right? About to get some rest?"

"That was the plan," Dillon said, taking a shortcut across one of the playing fields and heading for the gate leading out of the park.

"We're on Glasnevin Avenue, you can't miss it. The fire brigade is here and…"

"The fire brigade?"

"Someone set a car on fire."

"You sure McCabe wants me there? I'm home no more than twenty minutes after working that cash-in-transit robbery through the night."

"He specifically requested that you grace us with your presence. Look, it's a grey Volkswagen Bora that's been torched. We're thinking it's the vehicle that was used in the van robbery."

"I'm there in ten minutes," Dillon said, and started running with Lucifer along his side.

Actually, it took them ten minutes to make it home. He put Lucifer in the back of the car and climbed in. Amazingly, the Corsa groaned to life on the first try. The sun had disappeared and it had started to mist, again, as he headed for Glasnevin Avenue. The mist was just enough so that you had to turn on the wipers about every forty-five seconds.

Once he pulled onto Glasnevin Avenue he could see the smoke rising in the distance. Three stoplights later he was there, and pulled over to the curb. As he climbed out of the car, Lucifer jumped into the front seat, ready to go along. Dillon closed the car door and the dog looked ready to begin barking, saw what was left of the smoking vehicle, and apparently decided he'd be just fine waiting in the car.

Uniformed Garda were busy keeping the small crowd at a distance. Farther down the road, a car with flashing lights seemed to be diverting gawking traffic. Dillon headed toward the smoking vehicle. He flashed his ID to one of the uniforms minding the small crowd, slipped beneath the "DO NOT CROSS" barrier, and a moment later got his gracious welcome from Inspector McCabe.

"It's about time," he said, turning to face Dillon, then he turned round again and continued to watch the firemen send more foam into what was left of the burned out vehicle. "I'd say we found our vehicle, or what's left of it," McCabe said without actually looking at Dillon.

"Why here? Why not somewhere out in the country? Or why not just drive it into the ocean? We're on an island, for Christ's sake."

"Hmm-mmm, no nap yet, Dillon?"

"No, not yet, anyway. And wouldn't there seem to be a thousand different ways to dispose of a vehicle besides setting it on fire on a busy city street in the middle of the day?"

"One would certainly think so, particularly after the fact, it's been," McCabe looked at his watch, "over sixteen hours since the robbery. It's almost as if they're toying with us."

"Toying with us?"

"Letting us know they aren't too worried about getting caught. Bastards think they've already gotten away with it."

"My limited experience tells me this is not the way Eddie Fleming would operate. He wouldn't take the risk, it's stupid."

"Yes, I would agree. I spoke with Simmons, just a bit earlier, he covered your brief conversation with this Tommy O'Brien person. You have anything to add? How did he seem?"

"O'Brien? I'd say he's one lucky boy. Paddy Dunne takes a round and doesn't make it while Tommy takes three and is sitting up in bed, eating bacon strips the next morning. He had a very rough description of a woman or some guy dressed as a woman who apparently stopped them. The concept is clever enough to be Eddie Fleming, but the description, loose as it was, didn't match. Fleming stands six feet even with bright blue eyes, Tommy O'Brien didn't click on either one of those points. I can't put my finger on it, but it didn't sound right."

"You learn anything on Fleming's prison escape?" McCabe asked.

"Fleming's, no, but it's just a little after six in the morning in the States. I'll contact them in a bit and should have some information relatively soon, maybe even today, regarding circumstances."

The fire brigade was hosing the vehicle down with water now. Clumps of foam and burnt upholstery flooded out the open doors, onto the pavement, and down Glasnevin Avenue toward a sewer. The smoke

64

was all but gone, and what remained was just a burned out hulk.

"Shall we have a look?" McCabe said, then stepped toward the car without waiting for Dillon's response.

The term "charred" didn't seem to do justice to the interior remnants of the four-door vehicle. Just the metal frames of the seats remained, the upholstery having literally gone up in smoke. What there was of the dashboard consisted of nothing more than some wires and bits of fused plastic. The door panels had disappeared. The brake pedal consisted of a metal frame with the charred remains of the rubber pad. The gas pedal was completely gone. The exterior was scorched, but there were a few areas that appeared relatively unaffected. It would be interesting to see if they could pull a match from the paint chips the forensic team had gathered out at the Weston Airport earlier that morning. Any hope of fingerprints or traces of DNA seemed like a wishful fantasy. All in all it looked like slim pickings.

"Another piece to the puzzle or a completely new puzzle?" McCabe asked, and looked at Dillon.

He didn't have an answer.

# **Chapter Thirteen**

**Lucifer was asleep in** the front passenger seat when Dillon eventually returned to the Corsa. The small crowd was gone. What little traffic there was seemed to be moving just fine. The Corsa started almost immediately, and they pulled a U-turn in the middle of the street and headed for home.

Once inside, Dillon turned on his computer and emailed a former workmate back in the States, asking for any information on Eddie Fleming's escape. Then he turned off his phone, climbed into bed, pulled the covers up and fell into a deep sleep. Lucifer woke him just a little after four.

Dillon let him out in the back garden, put the coffee on, then hopped in the shower for a good twenty minutes. He was on his second cup of coffee when he remembered his email request. He fired up his computer, and there was a one-and-a-half-page report on Eddie Fleming's escape, along with a note that said he owed his friend dinner and drinks next time he was back in town.

It seemed while in prison, Fleming, not for the first time, requested a meeting with his court-appointed attorney. Ostensibly, the purpose of the meeting was to discuss a plea strategy in an upcoming appeal case. Somehow, during the meeting he drugged his attorney, changed into the attorney's clothes, then simply walked out of the room, leaving the attorney passed out at the table with an orange prison jumpsuit draped over his shoulders. Fleming waved the attorney's ID badge through four separate monitored stations where no one bothered to question him, and he basically just walked out of federal prison. Authorities surmised he may have boarded a bus or hailed a cab. He hadn't been seen in almost six months. So much for security.

Dillon made a sandwich for a quick meal, filled a thermos with coffee, then debated about leaving Lucifer at home. In the end, he acquiesced and brought him to the office. He left him locked in the car with a chew toy, a dog biscuit and his blanket, and headed into the office.

His desk seemed to still remain the collection point for empty tea mugs, and he dutifully grabbed four of the things off his desk, deposited them in the break room sink, then sought out McCabe.

He found him in his office, along with four other individuals, Simmons, Sean Flynn, and two guys he recognized from last night, but whose names he had already forgotten, again. He knocked on the door frame.

"Thank you for joining us, Marshal Dillon. You received our phone message after all."

Actually no, he didn't. Probably because he'd turned his phone off when he finally crawled into bed, and forgot to turn it back on until just now. But, he didn't tell McCabe that.

"Thought you might be interested in this," Dillon said, and handed the page-and-a-half report he'd printed off on Fleming's escape across the desk to McCabe. "I can sum it up for you if you'd like, save time."

"Please, by all means."

"He somehow drugged his court-appointed attorney, switched clothes and just walked out of the prison facility, hasn't been seen since. So much for American federal security." That last line brought some not so subtle laughter from the assembled.

McCabe drummed his fingers on the desk and seemed to be deep in thought. He turned in his chair, leaned back and stared at the ceiling for a moment. A series of quick glances shot back and forth among the five people waiting on the far side of the desk for the other shoe to drop.

"So we've got one man dead, another wounded, two-point-five million euros missing, and a burned out vehicle. We've no idea who was involved, and no idea where they might be, or even how many, although we've been led to believe there were two vehicles involved."

"I'm having my calls being screened, because between the superintendent, the minister for public safety, the legal department at Ulster Bank, bloody damned reporters and Eamon Dunne, my phone has been ringing off the hook. Now, does anyone have anything positive to add?"

No one said anything.

"Very well, then go out there and find something. I can't believe these bastards have simply disappeared."

No one moved for a long moment.

"Well?" McCabe half-shouted.

Suddenly they were all up and heading out the door. Once out of McCabe's office, everyone headed in a different direction, the task being to simply get away from McCabe as quickly as possible.

# Chapter Fourteen

**As soon as they** were out of McCabe's office, Dillon hurried to his desk and turned his cellphone back on.

"You too?" a voice said from behind, and he turned to look at Simmons. "I turned mine off so I could catch a couple of hours' sleep and completely forgot until I pulled into the parking lot here."

"I was just getting ready to hit the sack when I got the call about the burning car on Glasnevin Avenue. What a waste of time that turned out to be. Maybe they'll get some paint chips, if we're lucky, but they sure as hell didn't need me there. Once I got back home I shut the cellphone off and then promptly forgot."

"It's bound to be something like that all day long. You have a plan?"

"A plan?" Dillon asked.

"I'm headed over to get a copy of the autopsy report on Paddy Dunne. Come on along, well, unless you've got something else scheduled."

Dillon gave a quick glance at the two calls that had been dumped into the message center on his phone, one from this office, probably alerting him to the meeting they'd just fled. The second message was from his sometime friend with benefits, Abbey. Not that he wouldn't love to set something up with her, but unfortunately it was going to have to wait.

"So, can you join me?" Simmons asked.

"As long as you're driving."

They headed up to the north side of Dublin, wound their way through Broadstreet, Phibsboro, Cross Guns, and into Glasnevin, where Dillon currently lived.

Simmons took a right onto Griffith Ave, then said, "The Morgue used to be just a block or two away from the Customs House. I think they closed that facility in the late nineties. Typical, they had all sorts of grand plans to put it out in Marino, just off the Malahide Road. Turned into just one more victim of the Celtic Tiger crash when that brought everything down in 2009, and the plan got scrapped. It was a brutal couple of years that followed, looking at bodies in porta-cabins, pretty damn wretched."

"This facility we're heading to, it used to be Whitehall Garda Station. Another victim of the crash and all the budget cuts that came with it, now it's the Dublin morgue. How fitting. And here we are," Simmons said. He pulled to the curb in front of a dark blue Mercedes, and parked in another no-parking zone.

The morgue was a substantial, two-story brick building that sat on the busy intersection of Griffith Ave and Drumcondra Road. Situated behind a black, wrought-iron fence, the building had large, attractive windows and a front door set at a forty-five-degree angle on one corner of the building. If you were just walking past you'd never be able to guess the business conducted inside.

Simmons sat behind the wheel for a moment, quietly drumming his fingers on the steering wheel.

"What are you thinking?" Dillon asked.

"I'm not sure. Something nagging me in the back of my mind about this, but I can't quite put a finger on it. What say we go in and maybe I'll find out," he said, and climbed out of the car.

# Chapter Fifteen

**Reggie wore a top** hat and a fancy black coat with tails just outside the Shelbourne Hotel. The coat was festooned with red epaulets, red lapels and a set of double-breasted silver buttons. In his black and white pinstripe trousers and shined shoes, he felt like a right proper gentleman.

He stood at the top of the steps with his arms clasped behind his back, and smiled at passersby. Occasionally someone would climb the steps to enter the Shelbourne and he would gracefully hop over to the door, open it, then take a low bow and say, "Welcome to the Shelbourne, the finest hotel in Dublin." On rare occasions they would ignore him, but usually they grinned. Sometimes they shrugged their shoulders and giggled and thought, *So this is how the other half lives.*

He spotted the taxi from halfway down the block. Just in case he wasn't sure, the driver had flashed his lights to confirm. Reggie made his way down the front stairs, timing his arrival at curbside just as the vehicle came to a halt. He opened the passenger door and gave a gracious bow as the lady, in a very unladylike pose, slid out of the back seat, then staggered a step or two in an effort to regain her balance on the sidewalk.

*A bit early to be on the piss*, Reggie thought, but maybe they'd been at a party, or for that matter a funeral.

She was attractive in a naughty sort of way, with short blonde hair, nearly white, and a well-endowed chest. Her dress looked too small, and even sober she would have seemed to have an edge to her. She looked around, trying to get her bearings, failed, then turned to the man in the backseat paying the driver.

"Hurry up, damn it. I need a drink."

The driver ignored her. The man in the back seat exhaled in response, then climbed out of the taxi and walked to the rear of the vehicle. The driver was right behind him, flashed a smile, opened the trunk and began to set a number of pieces of luggage on the curb.

There were five pieces of luggage altogether, two nondescript black bags one looking more battered than the other, a large, Louis Vuitton suitcase with what looked like a price tag still attached to the handle, and two grey cases, almost industrial in their appearance.

The grey cases appeared to be devoid of any pockets or zippers on the outside. The edges were squared at sharp right angles, and the corners appeared to be almost pointed. Each case featured a handle of black leather and some sort of elaborate combination device just beneath the handle. They appeared to be barely half the size of the Louis Vuitton affair.

Reggie closed the passenger door once the woman staggered out of the way. She was just in the process of yelling, "Watch where you're bleedin' going," at a passerby who thankfully ignored her. Reggie hurried to the rear of the taxi and began to move the luggage onto the brass cart a bellboy had just rolled onto the sidewalk. Best to get the bitch off the sidewalk and checked in before she assaulted someone.

He hoisted the Louis Vuitton up onto the cart first, gave a silent groan at the weight of the thing, confirmed that it was indeed a price tag hanging from the handle, then reached for one of the grey industrial-looking cases.

"Leave those, I'll take them," the man said. He was American, maybe six feet tall with sparkling blue eyes. As he spoke he palmed a five-euro note and handed it to Reggie. Reggie quickly slipped the note into his trouser pocket with a practiced move, smiled, then reached for one of the black bags. Once he loaded the second black bag he nodded at the bellboy, who rolled the cart in through a lower door and up an inside ramp.

The man grabbed a grey case in either hand and headed up the stairs, ignoring the woman. Reggie hurried past him and up the steps, grabbed the polished brass handle on the massive door, pulled it open and bowed.

"Welcome to the Shelbourne, sir. The finest hotel in Dublin."

"Thanks," he said, and headed into the lobby.

At this point the woman was halfway up the steps, pulling herself along the brass rail using both hands.

Experience had taught Reggie that an offer to assist would likely be met with an explosion of some sort followed by a raging string of invectives hurled in his general direction, and so he simply maintained his post, holding the door. She made it to the top of the stairs, seemed to take a deep breath and aimed for the open door.

"Welcome to the Shelbourne," he said as she staggered past.

For a brief moment she looked like she was going to respond, but then thankfully forgot whatever had been on the tip of her tongue and continued forward.

Happy to have her inside and someone else's problem, Reggie closed the door and resumed his post at the top of the stairs, smiling with his arms clasped behind his back.

Inside, the gentleman was in the process of receiving the cards that would serve as his room key. He smiled, thanked the woman behind the front desk, then nodded at the young man waiting next to the brass cart with their luggage.

"Hang on just a minute," Reggie said.

He walked over to the couch and two chairs positioned along the wall opposite the front desk. The woman was asleep in the chair, with her legs stretched onto the couch. She was snoring, and as he drew closer he noticed she was drooling ever so slightly. Not for the first time, he made a mental note of, *Never, ever, again,* then gently shook her shoulder.

She wrinkled her nose, but not in a cute way, groaned then pushed his hand away.

He shook her shoulder again, this time just a bit more forcefully, looking around as he did so. Fortunately, no one, including the bell boy, seemed to be paying any attention to them.

"Get the fuck away from me. Just let me sleep and I'll do you all later," the woman groaned.

"Noreen, I've got plenty of whiskey for you up in the room. All you can drink, and a nice bed where you can sleep as long as you want."

"Ummm," she half-groaned, then gave just the slightest hint of a smile. Her eyes gradually blinked open and she looked at him. "More to drink?"

"As much as you want. Come on now, let me help you up," he said, taking hold of her arm and helping her to her feet. She was going to need assistance, a lot of assistance, getting to their suite. He waved the bellboy over. Against his better judgement, he turned the grey, industrial cases over to him. "Put these on your cart and I'll help her get to the room. It was a long flight," he added as an afterthought, already knowing that the ruse would never work.

The bellboy nodded, but didn't respond. He'd seen around her Dublin before, somewhere in the city, though never in the Shelbourne. The call girls here were of a much higher class.

They made their way across the lobby and around a corner. They walked down the hallway and through a set of double doors with beveled glass. On the far side of the doors the hallway widened and grew just a bit more elegant. Oil paintings in heavy gilt frames featuring Dublin landmarks adorned the walls.

"Just around the corner, sir," the bellboy said over his shoulder.

A good ten feet behind him, the man guided the drunken woman with both hands, all the while keeping his eyes focused on the two industrial cases riding along with the luggage. Thankfully, other than asking, "How much farther?" a half-dozen times, her mumblings remained incoherent.

He rounded the corner just as the bellboy pushed the cart against the wall and turned to face him. "I'll need your key, sir."

He braced the woman against the wall, then pinned her in place using his left arm. He fumbled in his suit coat pocket for a moment before he was able to hand the plastic card over. The bellboy opened the door, then stepped inside and held it so the two of them could enter. He guided the woman across the gracious sitting room and headed for the bedroom, calling, "You can just leave the luggage by the door."

He walked her into the closest bedroom, helped her just past the bedroom door, then let go of her arm and left her to her own devices. She staggered forward a few paces, misjudged the distance to the four-poster bed, bounced off the edge of the elegant bed and landed on the floor with a loud, "Oomph."

He left her there and hurried out to the main room just as the bellboy was setting the Louis Vuitton onto the floor. "Is there anything else you'll be needing at the moment, sir?"

"No, no, all very good, thank you, thank you," the man said, handing a five-euro note to the bellboy, then opening the door in an effort to speed him on his way.

# **Chapter Sixteen**

**There was a sort** of receptionist counter in the small lobby of the morgue. The counter rested behind a glass partition built into the wall. An older woman sat behind the counter, tapping keys on a computer keyboard. She seemed to speed up a bit as Simmons and Dillon approached, maybe attempting to finish the sentence or paragraph she was typing before they interrupted her progress.

She raised her hands with a flourish, then looked up and said, "Well, will you look what the cat dragged in."

"Hello, Madeline. How you keeping?"

"Couldn't be better, Simmons. You're here for the Dunne family?"

"Not exactly, just need a copy of the report, maybe a short conversation with whoever performed the autopsy and we're on our way."

"They'll be finishing up with the family member shortly. You can have a seat. Care for a cuppa?"

"No, thank you," Simmons replied, then said, "A family member?"

"A brother." Madeline looked left and right then half-whispered, "Bit insistent if you ask me."

Simmons nodded, and stepped over toward some chairs lined up against the wall. "Sounds like Eamon Dunne might be back there. Best not to say anything other than offer condolences. I've a feeling…"

The security door leading to the rest of the building suddenly flew open and bounced off the wall with a loud bang. Eamon Dunne charged into the lobby like a steam locomotive followed by his solicitor, Tully McBride.

"I'd be a right bloody fool if I couldn't…" He stopped in mid-rant and looked at Simmons and Dillon. "You'd better hope to Christ you find the bastards who did this to me brother before I do, or so help me God," he said, then looked like he was about to say more, thought better of it, and stormed out of the building.

"Gentlemen," McBride said, and nodded by way of acknowledgement. He paused for a moment, waited for a comment or maybe a question, then smiled coldly and followed Dunne out the door.

"I think it's probably safe to go in now. You might be able to catch Doctor Byrne in viewing room three," Madeline called from behind the glass partition once Dunne and his solicitor left.

She pushed a button somewhere, and the door buzzed. Dillon heard a lock snap and Simmons pulled the door open. They walked down a short hall, past white metal doors labeled "Viewing Room One" and "Viewing Room Two". The smell of disinfectant mixed with some sort of industrial air freshener grew stronger the farther down the hall they walked. Simmons pushed the third door open and they stepped into a small, empty, antiseptic room.

The room had more of a pine scent to it, and seemed just large enough to hold no more than five or six people. The wall facing them had a large window. On the other side of the window stood an attractive, dark-haired woman with piercing blue eyes, and looking sexy in a white lab coat. She smiled, gave a quick wave to Simmons and said, "Just give me a minute and I'll meet you out in the hall." Then she wheeled a gurney out through a door. The gurney was covered with a pressed white sheet. The vague form of a body beneath was identifiable, and then of course the two feet sticking up. Presumably it was Paddy Dunne arranged beneath the starched white sheet.

Out in the hall, Dillon couldn't seem to shake the pine scent. Simmons said, "So what'd you think of your friend, Mr. Dunne?"

"Suitably upset. Hard to see it as an act, I'd guess he was probably caught off-guard running into the two of us. Tell you the truth, I'm more than a little surprised he even recognized us."

"We've had dealings in the past. Not one to trifle with."

"Dealings?"

"Nothing that ever stuck. How can I put it? The expressway eventually leads to him, we just never seem to be able to find the entrance."

"Expressway?"

"Always seems to be linked to gambling, illegal cigarettes, automobile parts shipped to Syria…"

"Syria?"

"Yeah. Of course, nothing the least bit fishy on that count. He's a careful bastard, I'll give him that much. At the end of the day, and there were a lot of days, he would always be just one step out of reach. This one though, his brother getting killed. I can't believe it was planned, at least not the way it ended. I'd say there's a good chance whoever is involved, if he has the slightest hint as to who was killed, he's got to be running for his life right now. There's an awfully good chance we're in a race to find him before the likes of Eamon Dunne gets hold of him."

"If he's got that sort of past history, how is it he's delivering cash to banks?"

"Eamon Dunne? Welcome to Ireland, Dillon. Friends in high places for one thing. The other is that up until 2014 the cash-in-transit deliveries were more or less secured by two armed Garda and four to eight lads with the Home Defense Force. It ran the banks close to the tune of fifty million euros annually for the privilege. Then, in 2014, their accounting departments decided that was an unnecessary expense, and you saw the result of that decision last night. It used to be that the mere threat of Eamon Dunne involved was all the protection the banks needed, well, up till now that is."

A door down the hall opened and the woman they'd seen a few minutes ago stepped out and called, "Simmons, up here. Come on, will ya? I'm dying for a tea."

# Chapter Seventeen

**They hurried down the** hall, Simmons talking to her before they were halfway there. "Alicia, this is the infamous Marshal Dillon, an American detailed to us in the hopes we can straighten him out. Sadly he's going to take a lot of work. Marshal, meet the famous Doctor Byrne."

"Oh, just ignore him, Marshal. He doesn't know when to stop," she said, and held out her hand.

Dillon shook her hand. She gave a firm grip and looked him in the eye. He said, "Please, call me Jack, Doctor."

"Only if you call me Alicia. Now, tell me, who'd you piss off to get stuck with Simmons this afternoon?"

"The list is long," Dillon said, and she laughed.

"Come on, Simmons is going to be buying us tea. It's the least he can do, under the circumstances," she said.

"Throw in a copy of Paddy Dunne's autopsy report and it's a deal, and since I'm feeling generous, the two of you can share a chocolate."

"Already done," she said as she turned and led them down the hall toward a door labeled "Office." As they walked, she reached into a pocket of her lab coat and handed a folded report to Simmons.

"This is just the initial report, blood tests and things will be a couple of days. Heavy-caliber round, just the one, fired at close range. One in a million shot. The bullet entered via his armpit on the left side, just missing his protective vest. It basically took out his lung, clipped his aorta and shattered his th3, that's the Thoracic spine, as it exited the body."

She glanced at the two of them for comment, but none came.

"In short, he didn't have a chance. If death wasn't instantaneous, it couldn't have been anymore than sixty seconds away."

"So what you're saying is the first responders on the scene couldn't have done much to save him."

She shook her head. "He could have been shot on the table in the operating room and they wouldn't have been able to save him."

She pushed her way through a door, and they entered a larger room with industrial grey carpet. A half-dozen offices, barely large enough for a desk and chair, were strung out along the walls with an equal number of blue office cubicles in the center of the room. Two of the offices were occupied as well as all six of the cubicles. Alicia led them past the cubicles, through another door, and into a break room.

The break room had a candy machine that featured M&M's, chocolate bars, bags of potato chips, and boxes of what looked like some sort of jelly candy. The sink sported the minimum standard of four dirty mugs, at least two of which had lipstick stains. Alicia walked over to a tea-dispensing machine and said, "You'll need two euros, Simmons, well, unless you're having one, too, in which case you'll need three."

"None for me," Dillon said.

"I think I'll pass, too," Simmons said.

"Okay, suit yourselves, although I can't say that I blame you, pure raunch coming out of this dreadful unit," Alicia said.

She grabbed a one-euro coin from Simmons' outstretched hand, inserted it into the tea dispenser and pressed two buttons. A paper cup dropped more or less in place, the machine whirred, and a disgusting looking diarrhea-like sludge drained into the cup. A layer of foam rose up inside the cup, stopped just at the rim, letting you think it was finished just before a final excretion suddenly shot out of the machine, causing foam and tea to overflow and run down the sides of the cup.

"Damn it, I hate it when that happens, and it happens every bloody time," she said, sounding genuinely upset. She pulled the cup from the machine, then hurried over to a small round table, crying, "Ouch, whoa that's hot, damn it, ouch."

"Now that was worth a euro," Simmons laughed.

She took a sip from her cup and grimaced. "Oh, God, yuck. So, tell me, was the family member for Paddy Dunne who I thought it was?"

"Depends on who you thought it was?"

86

"Himself. Eamon Dunne. God, it was him, wasn't it? He looks just like he does when he's on the news. This was the cash-in-transit robbery, right?"

Simmons nodded.

"Your man Eamon was more than a little upset. I wouldn't want to be on the receiving end of that temper."

"Understandably," Simmons said. "You come across anything out of the ordinary in your autopsy?"

"No, given the circumstances. Pretty sure it was a hollow-point round. The size of the exit wound was massive."

"Distance?"

"Based on the powder burns? I'd estimate the distance at less than a foot. The shooter had to have been right next to him. With a little more study, if we find out it was, oh, say six inches, that wouldn't really surprise me."

Dillon was thinking back to Tommy O'Brien's description, about the individual with the American accent. "She just started shooting," Tommy had said, describing Paddy Dunne's last's few seconds.

Paddy Dunne was hit with a hollow point round and killed almost immediately. Tommy O'Brien is sitting up eating breakfast with a smile a little more than twelve hours later. Were there two shooters? But Tommy O'Brien seemed pretty insistent that the woman, or whatever it was, was supposedly the only shooter. Two weapons? A second shooter?

"...not uncommon," Alicia was saying. "The shock hits them, you'd be surprised how many people hold out hope that there's been some dreadful mistake. We've all seen it on the TV. Some innocent with a marvelous figure in a sexy dress comes in to identify the body and it's not her brother or her boyfriend, at which point her cellphone rings and the one she's there to identify is calling her with a dinner invite. But that's only on the telly. I've to say, in my twelve years here, I've never seen it happen. I don't think anyone could ever be that lucky coming here. So Mister Dunne's reaction is par for the course."

"The difference is there's a very good chance his threat can be carried out," Simmons said.

They chatted on for another few minutes, or more accurately, Alicia and Simmons continued talking. Dillon couldn't quite drag himself from Tommy O'Brien's version of things not quite adding up.

"So, what'd you think?" Simmons asked a few minutes later. They were just heading out the black wrought-iron gate outside the Dublin morgue.

"I thought she was very attractive, and I loved how she made you pay for the tea."

Simmons looked at Dillon, smiled then shook his head.

"I'm puzzled," Dillon said.

"How so?"

"The facts as we know them, or rather heard them, don't seem to match the facts Alicia presented and Paddy Dunne's wound."

"Gee, you mean someone's lying?"

"Possibly. Once the shooting starts, it's hard to keep things straight. What if an individual did exactly what

Tommy O'Brien said, and someone else, with a heavier-caliber weapon, pops in the other door and shoots Paddy Dunne. Tommy O'Brien's already been shot two, maybe three times, maybe he's unconscious, maybe he's frightened, make that scared to death. Maybe he's had a lapse of memory and he's just filling in the blanks and trying to make us happy. It wouldn't be the first time something like that happened."

"That works except that Paddy Dunne was shot on the left side, just beneath his arm and presumably from a distance of less than a foot. So, either the shooter reached across Tommy O'Brien and pulled the trigger while Paddy was completely turned around. Or, maybe Tommy did and he's our inside man," Simmons said.

He walked around to the driver's side of the vehicle, looked past the no-parking zone where they were parked to the empty space behind them where the blue Mercedes had been. "You think that was Eamon Dunne's Mercedes parked in that spot behind us?"

"Would it make a difference?"

"It'd be nice to be ahead of the bastard once in awhile, even if it's just for a parking place."

# __Chapter Eighteen__

**They were headed across** the city to the Slándáil
Transit office. Simmons was on the phone with
McCabe, explaining the apparent discrepancy with
Tommy O'Brien's version of events. Dillon was
listening to half the conversation.

"No, sir, I didn't mean that. I'm not suggesting the
man is lying, sir. It's just one of those sort of loose ends
I think we should tie up. Before we go back and talk to
him I'd like to look at the employment records,
O'Brien's in particular, but everyone else as well. I
mean an Eamon Dunne business, you'd think there
might be a number of names that could ring a bell. Yes.
No. No, not for a few more days. We've got the
preliminary report, now just waiting for the blood work
up and that sort of thing to come back. She did, said if it
wasn't instantaneous he probably didn't have more than
sixty seconds." He glanced over at Dillon and nodded.
"Right. If you would sir, that would speed things up,
yes, thank you. We'll give them a bit of time. Yes, sir,"
he said and disconnected.

"Change of plans?" Dillon asked.

"Not really. He's placing a call to Slándáil Transit. Giving them the 'it's just standard procedure' line on the employment records. With any luck we'll be able to walk in and pick up the files. Then it's back to the office, where a group of us will wade through the records. I just want to give them a bit of time to get things sorted. No sense in spending a minute more than necessary while under the watchful eye of Eamon Dunne."

They pulled into the petrol station maybe ten minutes later and gassed up, then drove around the corner to a subway shop, grabbed a couple of sandwiches and ate them leaning against the car in the parking lot.

"We'll give 'em another fifteen or twenty minutes to pull the files. God, but I don't want to wait around in Eamon Dunne's company any longer than I have to. And if I know McCabe, he'll expect us to be working the midnight shift, doing an initial peruse of those files."

As if on cue, Dillon's cellphone rang. He pulled it out of his pocket and looked, Abbey. He thought long and hard about answering the call, but all he'd be able to tell her was he had to work and they wouldn't be able to get together tonight. It figured, the one time he couldn't…

"You going to answer that?" Simmons asked on the sixth or seventh ring.

"Wish I could. A friend with benefits, but if we're going to be working tonight, probably through the night, what's the point?"

"Now that's what I call real dedication. Or just plain stupidity, I'm not sure which is correct."

"I think the stupidity part. She can be *very* good."

They pulled into the gate at Slándáil Transit twenty minutes later, and flashed ID's to a grumpy-looking guard in need of a shave. He took his time looking at the ID's, examining first Simmons' picture then looking at Simmons, then back to the ID just to be sure. He did the same thing with Dillon, seeming to enjoy wasting their time. Finally he handed Dillon's ID back and said, "Mr. Dunne's been waiting on yas, and he ain't what you'd call happy."

"We'll be sure to tell him you took your sweet time," Simmons said. Just as the guard started to respond, Simmons just pulled away. "This should be fun," Simmons said and followed up with a groan.

He pulled into the handicapped spot opposite the front door. The building was a two-story, white-stucco affair with what looked like a slanted tin roof. The name "Slándáil Transit" ran across the front of the building in six-foot-high yellow neon letters. Four heavy-duty vans, duplicates of the one involved in last night's incident, were parked off to the side. One of the vans was up on blocks that were wedged under the front end. Two guys in blue, one-piece overalls were in the process of wrestling a tire off the front passenger side of the van.

"Okay, the sooner you go in, the sooner you can get the hell out of here," Simmons seemed to say to himself, then took a deep breath and opened the car door.

They entered through a set of double doors, dark blue wooden frames with large tinted glass panels and brass handles. They stood in a small entryway just beyond the front doors. All four walls in the entryway appeared to be lined with half-inch steel. What looked like a space-age version of a chrome pay phone was set in the wall. The phone had just one button to push, and it was labeled "push."

Simmons looked at Dillon, sort of shrugged as he pushed the button, and the screen slowly came to life. A woman's image suddenly appeared.

"May I help you?" she said. The audio wasn't quite in sync with the movement of her lips.

"Garda Síochána here to pick up some employment records," Simmons said.

"Thank you. I'll alert them to your arrival," she said, and then the screen suddenly went blank.

Not more than a minute later there was a loud buzz and a metal door off to the side opened. A burly guy with a shaved head and a flattened nose pushed a green, two-wheeled dolly stacked with four boxes. He was wearing a grey suit coat that looked two sizes too small, and a dark blue t-shirt with yellow embroidery that read, "Slándáil Transit," just like the vans. Behind him stormed Eamon Dunne, eyes glaring, red-faced and looking like he'd gladly tear your head off.

"You two? Well it's about fecking time. These are employment files going back to the year two-thousand. I'll expect 'em back in the order given as soon as you're finished. Mousey'll load 'em up for yas. I'll expect to learn anything you find the moment you find it. Are we clear?"

Simmons said, "That's not gonna…" But Dillon put his arm out to stop him before he could say anything else.

"Mr. Dunne, first of all, let me say how truly sorry I am for the loss of your brother Paddy. I know words can't express. I also want you to know, regardless of past history or what you may think, we're putting our full effort into finding the individual or individuals involved. We'll follow the trail wherever it leads, sir."

Dillon seemed to have caught Dunne off-guard, and he fidgeted for a moment, unsure exactly how to respond.

"American?"

"Yes, sir, I'm a US Marshal. There's an outside chance, slim at best, that an American may have been involved. We haven't found any proof of that yet, but I'm going to keep looking. We'll leave no stone unturned. If he's involved, we'll get him, and again, sir, I'm sorry for your loss."

"What's your name?"

"Dillon, Jack Dillon, sir."

"And you're working with the Garda?"

"Yes, I am. They, or rather we, all want to get whoever did this just as badly as you, sir."

He nodded for a moment, then seemed to recover and looked at Simmons. "You and your lot could stand to learn a thing or two from this man, ya knacker." Then he turned on his heel, flashed some sort of card in front of a small screen next to the door so that the lock clicked, and stormed back into the office.

"That's us right out the door," Simmons said to the thug with the two-wheeled dolly, as if the car marked "Garda Síochána" might have belonged to someone else.

"Yeah, and parked illegally in the handicapped spot. Figures," Mousey growled. He wheeled the dolly out to the rear of their car, then loaded the four boxes into the trunk. Each and every time he bent down to pick up a box he shot a disgusted look their way.

"Gee, we can't thank you enough, Mousey." Simmons smiled once he'd finished loading the boxes into the rear of the car.

"Aw, feck yas, feck the both of yas," Mousey growled, then headed back into the building.

"Thanks for including me," Dillon said.

"So, well done, you," Simmons said, looking Dillon up and down. "Now you've got a brand new friend in Dublin. One of the most crooked, deceitful, awful, fecked-in-the-head bastards to ever walk the face of the earth, none other than the wanker of all wankers, Eamon Dunne."

# Chapter Nineteen

**Just on a whim** they started out with Tommy O'Brien's file and went through it as a group while everyone was relatively fresh. Unfortunately, they found nothing out of the ordinary. O'Brien had been employed by Slándáil Transit for close to six years. Prior to that he'd served four years in the Home Defense forces, including a tour in Lebanon in 2007 and another tour in Bosnia in 2009, earning the UN Peacekeeping medal, twice. He left the forces with the rank of private.

There were eight of them scattered around the break room, wading through the Slándáil Transit employment records. Everyone was feasting on cold pizzas and warm Cokes. They were tired, bleary-eyed, and based on the smell in the room, all in need of a hot shower. It was just after ten and they were maybe a third of the way through the files. Thus far they'd had a total of a big fat zero when it came to results. Simmons was holding the stage.

"So then he says, 'And Mr. Dunne, if you ever need your car washed or your big fat, hairy arse kissed, please, just call me. I'm your man, a US Marshal. All my mates call me Dildo, and for a very good reason, because I can give it to you anyway you like, whenever you like.'"

"So you've moved up in the world and you're friends with the rich and infamous, now, are ye, Dildo?"

"Just telling the man I was sorry for his loss. He was about to tear into Simmons, not that I wouldn't have enjoyed that, but I was anxious to get back here and share all this fun with you guys. Besides, Simmons had the car keys, and he only would have enjoyed me searching through his pockets."

"Thanks for putting a good light on all of us with that plonker Dunne," somebody said then followed up with a yawn.

It more or less went on like that for another four and a half hours, and at the end they hadn't learned anything more than when they started. It was almost three in the morning before Dillon made it out to his car.

Lucifer was waiting for him, looking out the driver's window. He'd barely opened the car door when the dog shot out between his legs, took the mandatory four steps and squatted. Only tonight he wouldn't even face Dillon, which maybe under the circumstances was fair. Once he finished he hopped back up on the driver's seat and then into the back, looking away from Dillon rather than acknowledging his presence.

When he got home Dillon followed the dog into the kitchen, opened the cupboard, made a show of pulling a dog biscuit out of the box and then tossed it onto the floor in front of him. The dog seemed to consider the offer for a moment.

"There you go, Lucifer. Come on, are we friends again?"

He seemed to scoff at the biscuit lying in front of him for a brief moment, then sniffed it, looked up at Dillon for a second or two before he wolfed the biscuit down in three quick bites and ran up the stairs. Dillon locked the front door and followed him up to the bedroom.

He tossed his clothes on a chair next to the bed. He climbed into the shower and stood there for a good five minutes, letting the steaming water run over him before he wandered back into the bedroom and crashed.

His cellphone ringing just before seven the following morning woke him. The ringing stopped just after the prescribed ten rings. He was in the process of drifting back to sleep when it started ringing again. He stumbled out of bed, kicked yesterday's shirt across the floor, picked up his trousers and pulled the cellphone out of the pocket just as it stopped ringing again. He checked his two missed calls. Both were from Abbey. He walked into the bathroom, then stumbled downstairs and placed a call to her once he had the coffee on.

"You okay? Jesus, I've been trying to reach you for a couple of days. Why didn't you call me back?" she said by way of answering.

"Yes, to your first question, I'm okay. Afraid I've been kind of busy the past couple of days. I know, I should have called, but it's been more than a little crazy working this case. The way things are going, I'm afraid I'll be tied up for the better part of the week."

"You're not trying to get rid of me?"

"No, Abbey, nothing like that. Actually, I'd like nothing better than to see you, believe me. But I'm due back in the office in little more than an hour. Right now I'm going on about three hours' sleep, and I wouldn't be the best of company. I'm sorry to put you off like that, but I…"

"Actually, I really wasn't calling to see you."

"Oh?"

"Yeah. I was sort of wondering if you could maybe help one of my friends out. She's been…"

"What's her problem?" It could be anything from car trouble to someone wanting their bedroom painted or her grass cut. Dillon suddenly wasn't really in the mood to find out right now.

"She got dumped by her boyfriend the other night and she wanted to talk to you."

Oh Christ, relationship counseling? First of all, he didn't want to do it. Second of all, he was horrible at it. His only advice would be to take the guy to bed and screw his brains out. "Talk to me?"

"Yeah, believe me, Mr. Not Very Sensitive and Caring, no one was more surprised than me. But she sort of, well, she insisted she wanted to talk to you, and so I told her I'd ask you. Although God only knows why I bother. I can see right now you're not in the humor to help."

He ignored that last line. "She have a joint bank account or own a car or a house with the guy? I'm not getting why she wants to talk to me. Is the guy American?" God, he didn't need this.

"Hello? Is anyone there even listening? I just told you, ya feck, she wouldn't tell me. I don't know what it's about. I just told her you were like a cop and she got like all secretive and everything and asked me to call you. Since then she's called, oh, just about every bleedin' hour on the hour to see if I talked to the likes of you yet. Hey Jack, you plonker, are you listening? Look, she's all upset, she's a dear friend of mine, and yes, I'll make it worth your while. Would you please just call her so I can get some peace and quiet and get me life back, for fecks sake."

# **Chapter Twenty**

**Once the offer to** make it worth his while came across, Dillon took down Abbey's friend's phone number, stuffed the note in his wallet, promising to call, and stepped into the shower in the hope of coming awake. He'd promptly forgotten about it by the time he stepped out of the shower. He made it into the office at just a little after nine. Everyone else on the investigative team looked just as exhausted as he felt.

They were herded into the break room to listen to McCabe's encouraging remarks where he labeled them as "*A bunch of pathetic wankers who had better pull the thumb out of their hole if they knew what was good for them!*" The fact that the break room was still littered with a dozen greasy pizza boxes and a half-dozen dirty tea mugs from the night before did nothing to improve the situation.

Simmons and Dillon took the encouragement to heart and fled the scene at the earliest opportunity with the idea they would talk again with Tommy O'Brien at John Connolly Hospital out in Blanchardstown.

"How do you want to handle this?" Simmons asked as he drummed his fingers on the steering wheel and stared out the car window. They were parked in the exact same no-parking zone as the previous day, and just now Simmons seemed more focused on the two women strolling past and heading toward the parking lot.

"I'm thinking we'll ask him the same questions as the last time. See if his answers differ. Hopefully, forty-eight hours after the fact, he's able to remember something that might help. Or he makes a mistake."

"Explain 'mistake'?" Simmons said.

"Just that feeling I can't seem to shake. Paddy Dunne takes one round and it leaves a hole in him you could drive a truck through. Tommy O'Brien takes three rounds, supposedly close-range, and he's sitting up in bed watching TV and eating bacon strips the next morning. He was pretty insistent there was only one shooter," Dillon said.

"Yeah, but under the circumstances, the stress, remember there was that vehicle that blocks them in from behind. Soon as that happens, the shooting starts. He may have blanked it out in his mind and he's just making it up, thinking he's helping us. I've seen it happen before."

"Yeah, maybe." Dillon said, and turned to face Simmons. "I don't want to accuse him of anything, but it's just not quite adding up in my mind."

"I don't know, let's see what he say's this morning." Simmons nodded as he opened his door. He pulled the antique cassette recorder out of the trunk. "You coming, or you gonna just sit there all day?" he said.

Dillon slowly climbed out of the passenger side, and they headed into the hospital.

They took the elevator up to the third floor, then wound their way through the maze of hallways to the nurses station outside Tommy O'Brien's room. Grania, the nurse who dispensed the breath mints to them the last time they were there, sat at the nurses station, working her way through a stack of files. She looked up and flashed a momentary fake smile as they approached.

"Here to see Tommy O'Brien. Okay if we go in?" Simmons said.

Grania nodded, then looked down at the open file in front of her and began to write something. She kept writing as she spoke. "He's being discharged later this afternoon. He'll probably have a final consultation with the doctor sometime after the noon hour then he's out of here."

"A fast recovery, must be a very lucky man, out in just a little more than forty-eight hours," Simmons said, and shot Dillon a look. If she noticed, Grania the nurse gave no indication.

The door to room 305 was almost, but not quite, closed. Simmons quietly pushed the door open and they stepped inside. The bed next to the door was still empty. They could see O'Brien, or at least the lower half of his body. He was wearing jeans with dark socks and light blue slip-on slippers that looked like some sort of disposable issue from the hospital. Based on the tags

103

discarded at the end of the bed, the jeans were new. The TV was on, this time with sound, although it was somewhat muted. O'Brien was talking to someone on the phone and apparently unaware they were in the room.

"No. I'm out of here today. Probably, but not until this afternoon by the time they're done wanking me around. Can't wait to get out. I plan to grab a takeaway from Macari's and I'll be at Kennedy's tonight. I'll let you buy me a pint. No, I'm tellin' you, just relax, she won't. I'm a free man. I put an end to it a few nights back. No, she was cramping my style. Besides, I've already got a lot better action out there than her and I intend to enjoy it. So, you better keep an eye on your lot," he laughed. "Thanks, but no. Not a bother, I'm going to taxi home. So you'll be there tonight?"

Simmons stepped around the half-drawn curtain and gave a little wave. Dillon followed just in time to catch a wide-eyed look of surprise on O'Brien's face. Along with his brand new jeans, he was wearing a pressed, long-sleeve button-down shirt. Although his arm was still resting in the sling, the shoulder couldn't have been too bad if he'd been able to slip into the shirt. *Speedy recovery*, Dillon thought again.

"Hey, Des, I'd better ring off. Some lads just in to review things with me. Yeah. No, I'm sure, but thanks for asking. Yeah. Right. All right, see you there," he finally said, then hung up.

"Mr. O'Brien, you're looking well. Sorry to be a bother. I hope we're not interrupting," Simmons said.

"No, it's good to see yas. I was wondering if you'd come by today. Did you hear? They're going to give me the okay this afternoon and I can go home." He beamed a genuine smile.

"No, didn't know that. You sure you wouldn't want to stay? We could put in a word and you could be here through the end of the week," Simmons joked.

O'Brien looked like he wasn't sure how to take that at first, then got a broad grin across his face and said, "Aw, go on, yas."

"Well, that's awfully good news for you. Your recovery seems to be going well, then?"

"It's coming along. I'll have to mind myself for some time. I'm going to have to be off work for a while, thinking maybe I might spend some time in the south of Spain. You know, long as I have to sit around I might as well do it in the sunshine with some pretty women to look at."

"Sounds like a plan," Simmons said. "And I'd have to admit, the scenery might be a bit better than here."

"You've been there, the beaches?"

"Afraid not, at least not yet. Maybe someday though, it's sort of on my list of things to do. Who knows? Say, mind if we ask you a few questions? Purely routine. What we find is, right about now, forty-eight hours or so, oftentimes people remember something, maybe just a little thing, may not even seem important-like, but it can sometimes help us out in our investigation."

"How's it going, the investigation?"

"How's it going," Simmons said, and seemed to think for a long moment. "Well, to be quite honest, it's moving rather slowly. Not all that unusual. We think we might have the vehicle you mentioned, the one that ran into you. But it was set on fire, and I doubt we'll be able to learn much if anything from it. We've not had word of anyone walking through Temple Bar area covered in red dye, so how should I put it? We continue to check and re-check. That's why we'd like to chat with you this morning."

"Chat away," Tommy said.

"Thank you," Simmons said, then placed the antique recorder on the tray table alongside the bed. He made a show of popping the lid and inserting the cassette. "We'll have this going in just a jiffy here. Now, Tommy, a lot of what we're gonna ask here is the same things we asked the other day. Just routine, not to worry, but like I said, right about now the slightest thing might just pop into your memory, a wedding ring, maybe a tattoo, maybe someone called out a name. You get where I'm going with this?"

"Yeah, sure, hopefully something will come out. I just want to get the folks that did this."

"All right then, sooner we get started the sooner you can be sitting in the sun, looking at all those pretty Spanish girls," Simmons said, and pushed the record button.

"That thing looks ancient. You ought to get something a little more up-to-date," O'Brien laughed.

"Well now, there you go. I have to tell you, working under the thumb of budget cuts for the past almost ten

106

years, not to mention the staff reductions we've had to face, you start adding it all up, it's a wonder we don't have to take the bus out here just to do this interview." Simmons made a show of straightening the recorder on the tray table. "Right. There now, looks as if we're ready to go. Let me start again by asking your name. Oh, and we're in room three-zero-five, John Connolly Hospital, Blanchardstown. All right, and if you'd state your name for us, please."

"Tommy O'Brien."

"And you're talking to us of your own free will, correct."

"Yes I am. Glad to help."

"And I'm Detective Simmons, and also with us is US Marshal Jack Dillon. Are you with us, Marshall?" Simmons half-joked.

"I'm here," Dillon said.

Tommy O'Brien gave a sort of snort and smiled. This was going to be fun.

# **Chapter Twenty-One**

**They talked with Tommy** O'Brien for the next forty-five minutes. That's the royal "they", actually Simmons did virtually all the talking. Dillon just listened and gave the occasional nod. O'Brien remained pretty much on-script, a few discrepancies, but when Simmons returned to them, O'Brien reverted to his initial descriptions from two days earlier. The interview began to head more in the direction of casual conversation, just two guys talking smart. They'd been talking Irish rugby when out of the blue O'Brien asked Dillon, "So when you heading back?"

It was a minor point, maybe. The phrasing. Not "How long you over?", but rather when was he leaving. They both caught it, Simmons and Dillon, and hoped they hadn't given away a reaction.

"A few more days. Tell you the truth, we thought there might be some American connection here, but it didn't pan out. I just have to tie up some loose ends, more budget paperwork sort of things than anything else. Then I'll be on a flight back to the States. Lovely country you got here. Wish I'd had some free time. I'd like to come back here sometime and actually see it."

That seemed to satisfy O'Brien, and he seemed to relax just a bit more. "Hope you have a safe flight home," he said, and flashed a big smile. "You got anymore questions?" he asked Simmons.

"Questions? No, nothing I can think of. Anything you can think of that you'd like to add?" Simmons asked.

"No, no, I don't think so. I've got your card here. If something comes up, if I remember anything else, I'll be sure to give you a call. Course, I might be calling from Spain with a cold beer in my hand."

"And a pretty señorita on your lap," Simmons said.

"I can only hope," Tommy said and laughed.

"Well, thanks, Tommy. We'll be leaving you to it, then. This is Detective Simmons concluding the interview with Thomas O'Brien," Simmons said, then turned off the recorder. They chatted about Spanish beaches for another brief minute, said their goodbyes once again and left the room.

They stopped outside at the nurses desk, but Nurse Grania was off somewhere, probably lecturing a patient or giving an enema. Neither one of them said anything as they walked along the hallway maze to the elevator. They were both deep in thought. Two women rode down on the elevator with them, so it wasn't until they were actually sitting in the car that Simmons finally asked, "Well, what'd you think?"

"I think he memorized his script pretty well. I didn't catch anything that would raise a flag and in a way that raises a flag. The little old lady disguise, with a gun, Jesus."

"Yeah, he didn't seem to miss a beat. Did you notice he never mentioned Paddy Dunne? The man is shot, murdered right next to him, and he never once mentioned the lad, never asked how he was."

"Of course, maybe he got the word. Could be someone told him. Hell, it could have been Eamon Dunne himself telling him for all we know," Dillon said.

"It's starting to smell to high heaven," Simmons said.

"Yeah, and there was something about that last question, when am I heading back? It was like he knew we were shut down."

Simmons nodded, seemed to think for a long moment. "He seemed a bit relieved once he heard your answer."

"The speedy recovery gets me," Dillon said. "He's making plans to be at a pub tonight. He's got fresh clothes on, new jeans, apparently able to get into a shirt even though he was shot in the shoulder and his arm just two nights ago."

"You know who we haven't spoken with? Whoever did the surgery the night of the robbery. Never dawned on me till just now, we blew right past them. Come on," Simmons said, and climbed back out of the car.

# Chapter Twenty-Two

**Forty-five minutes later** they were seated in a small office within the larger surgical section. Simmons and Dillon were in black leather chairs across the desk from Dr. Eoin Murphy. They were listening, wide-eyed, as he reiterated his information. "Gentlemen, it's just like I told you, we would have released Mr. O'Brien yesterday except he kept complaining about pain. To tell you the truth, I don't think he had any pain. I think he just enjoyed the medication."

"But he was wounded in the shoulder, right? The round passed through his shoulder, didn't it?"

"Passed through? Oh, good lord, no. No, that wasn't the issue at all. Mr. O'Brien just had a small sliver, two actually, that lodged in his shoulder. The fear was there may have been a perforated artery. Fortunately that wasn't the case. We removed the slivers, stitched him up, nine stitches by the way, seven interior, they'll dissolve of their own accord, and just the two exterior stitches which we'll remove when he returns on his follow-up visit. He'll barely have a scar from the incident. Quite a lucky lad under the circumstances."

"And when will that be, the follow-up visit?" Simmons asked.

"I'm sorry, I don't know exactly. A week, possibly two, depending on recovery time. He seems to be doing a remarkable job." The good doctor looked from Simmons to Dillon, then back to Simmons again. "Is there a problem here, gentlemen?"

"No, no problem, sir. Just trying to understand the damage. Mr. O'Brien was also wounded in the arm, was he not?" Simmons asked.

"Well, yes, but barely a graze. We simply cleaned the wound and applied an antibiotic cream."

"An antibiotic cream?" Dillon said.

"Well yes, it was really just more a case of stippling than anything else."

"Stippling?"

"Oh, 'stippling' simply refers to a type of tattooing caused by still-burning gunpowder residue hitting the skin."

"Was he grazed on the side of his head?"

"He had a wound there, but it wasn't from a bullet. I'd surmise he caught the side of his head on the vehicle door or possibly even the pavement. I seem to recall some grains of sand being cleaned out of the wound."

"How long was he in the surgical unit?"

"How long? Ummm, certainly no more than an hour. Any wound can be serious if untreated, fear of infection you understand, but as far as a severity factor, I'm sure we dealt with much more serious situations in the ER that evening, or any other evening for that matter. I'd say he was one lucky individual based on the results of his partner. Tragic, really, and so damn young," he said shaking his head.

"Yes, sir, he was lucky, very lucky. Listen, we appreciate your time, doctor," Simmons said, rising out of the chair. "You've been a big help in setting us straight."

"Glad to be of assistance. Damn horrid affair, your young man murdered."

"It is indeed, sir."

"Gad, it seems I'm asking myself what the country is coming to, a number of times, in any given week."

They shook hands all around, then walked back out to the car without comment. Once they were seated in the car, Simmons put the key in the ignition, then looked at Dillon and said, "I'm thinking there's a pretty good chance your man has been playing us."

"You mean he's the inside man?"

"Possibly. One of them at least. We need to talk to the first responders."

"They told me there was a lot of blood and they were really focused on Paddy Dunne, trying to save his life," Dillon said.

"A lot of blood. What if all the blood belonged to Paddy Dunne? What if Tommy O'Brien basically injured himself in an effort to make himself look wounded? What if…"

Dillon's cell phone suddenly rang. In a reflex reaction he pulled it out of his pocket and checked the screen. Abbey. He pushed a button and sent the call into his message center. "Sorry about that. You were saying?"

"I want to look at the statements again from the first responders, and then I want to talk to them."

# Chapter Twenty-Three

**They reviewed the statements** from the first responders back in the office, then put a call out for them to meet at the Leixlip Garda station on Station Road. It was a modern-looking, three-story brick building with a parking space they were able to grab right in front of the door. For a change it was a legal parking space.

Officers Michael Benson and Terry Reilly were waiting for them when they arrived. Reilly was the one Dillon had brought the cup of tea to the night of the robbery when he'd first arrived on the scene.

They were seated at a metal table with a grey linoleum sort of top in a claustrophobic little interview room. The room was painted a dark grey color, and if you weren't depressed before you entered, a minute or two sitting in there would certainly do the trick. Both men glanced nervously at the written copies of their statements lying on the table between Simmons and Dillon. Simmons picked up on the reaction immediately.

"Relax, lads, you've done nothing wrong. We're just trying to get a handle on the events of that evening and we wanted to ask you some questions."

"Should we have a union representative here?" Benson asked, sounding like he wasn't buying what Simmons had just said.

Simmons shrugged. "You can if you want. Maybe let us ask the questions, and if you feel like you want a representative here we can call for one. I personally don't think you're going to need it. But obviously it's your choice."

They looked at one another, Reilly looked over at Dillon and then at Benson again and shrugged.

"Okay," Benson said. "I guess we can try it without. But if we need one, no offense, but we're going to stop and wait till he gets here. Sorry, but you know how it is these days."

"Yeah, unfortunately I get it," Simmons said. "Thanks for being here, gentlemen. We wanted to ask you about the condition of the two wounded men. When you arrived, were they both in the van?"

"No," said Benson. "At least not exactly. The driver, he was halfway out of the van, sort of hanging out, lying on the pavement, but his legs were still in the van. The other one…"

"Paddy Dunne," Reilly interjected.

"Yeah, Dunne. He was in the passenger seat, leaning over toward the driver's side. God, there was so much blood. All over the interior of the van, and a big puddle on the floor. We pulled him out, laid him on the

116

pavement and tried to resuscitate him. Not sure he ever revived."

"I said in the statement I didn't know if he was dead or alive," Reilly added. "It's the God's honest truth. We opened his vest and were doing CPR on him, but every time we pushed on his chest more blood just squirted out of the wound. Christ almighty, it was like a fountain, it was."

"I had my hands over the wound, applying pressure to stop the blood, but it wasn't doing any good," Benson said.

From the answers they were giving and the looks on both their faces, Simmons and Dillon could see just going over the event was uncomfortable for both of them. They were both transported back to that night, trying to do the impossible.

"And the partner, where was he?"

"At first he was laying on the ground, then, while we were trying to save Dunne, he sort of halfway crawled over and sat up against the side of the van."

"He kept telling us to help Dunne, wouldn't let us look to him, just said he was okay, and to look after his partner."

"Was he bleeding?" Dillon asked.

"That's the funny thing," Benson said. "I was thinking about it in the middle of last night. I haven't been sleeping very well since all this happened."

"Me neither," Reilly said.

"Anyway, he had blood all over him, but he sort of didn't seem that fazed. I was thinking maybe adrenaline was just pumping him up."

"Blood was soaking his shirt. It was all down the side of his face," Reilly said with a far away look in his eye, like he was suddenly back at the scene the other night, kneeling in the parking lot.

"He had that scrape on the side of his head," Benson added.

"Wouldn't let us near him, just kept telling us to take care of his partner. God, he's one tough little bastard," Reilly said, then looked over at Benson, who nodded in agreement.

"Did he seem in any pain, Tommy O'Brien?" Dillon asked.

"Well, he had all that blood all over him, but he didn't seem to care, just kept telling us to work on Dunne, save him."

"Yeah, and then he'd tell Dunne that he was going to be okay. Told him to hang in there a number of times."

"Yeah," Reilly agreed. "He was oblivious to his own injuries. Kept telling your man help was on the way."

"What'd the paramedics do when they arrived?"

"I was never so glad to see them," Benson said. "They had Dunne up on a gurney almost immediately and hustled him into the back of the ambulance. One of them walked O'Brien over, right behind the gurney, loaded him into the ambulance and then they just sped out of the parking lot with the siren blaring."

"O'Brien need any help getting into the ambulance?" Simmons asked.

"Well, there was one of them next to him, big guy."

"Mick Collins. I kinda know him from back when I played hurling against the bastard, never gave an inch," Reilly said.

"But actually, now that you mention it, he seemed to be able to go along pretty well. Your man Collins had him by the arm. To be honest, I'm not really sure he needed any help."

Benson looked over at Reilly, who nodded in agreement, then said, "He seemed okay except for the blood all over his shirt. I mean, your man was soaked and his hands were covered. Side of his face was a bloody mess."

It went on like that for another ten minutes. The more they heard, the more convinced Dillon became that all the blood dripping off of Tommy O'Brien was probably from Paddy Dunne.

"Anything else either one of you would care to add?" Simmons asked.

They glanced at one another, shook their heads, then Benson asked, "Are we in any kind of trouble? We did the best we could, but the wound on Dunne, even if he'd been in a hospital with doctors instead of a parking lot with the two of us, I don't think they could have saved him."

"You're in no trouble," Simmons said. "To tell you the truth, results from the autopsy suggest he was most likely dead by the time you arrived. The bullet nicked an artery."

"And it took out a vertebra. You did your absolute best, and unfortunately it appears no one could have saved him," Dillon added.

Reilly just shook his head.

They said their goodbye's. Simmons made a point of stopping in to chat with their watch commander to let him know Benson and Reilly weren't in any sort of trouble, and in fact had done their level best in what was an impossible situation.

On the drive back to the office they were both in deep thought until Simmons swore at someone who cut in front of them, then slowed to a stop while the vehicle made a right-hand turn.

"You know, maybe it's just different personalities, but Tommy O'Brien is spending an extra day in the hospital watching TV, enjoying the pain meds and lining up friends to buy him a pint tonight at Kennedy's pub. Meanwhile, Benson and Reilly can't sleep at night because they're thinking about Paddy Dunne and wishing they could have saved him."

# Chapter Twenty-Four

**They were pulling into** the parking lot, more or less convinced Tommy O'Brien was the answer to just about all their questions on the Slándáil Transit robbery and the murder of Paddy Dunne.

"I say we wander into Kennedy's tonight and see what transpires. If O'Brien's involved he'll have to make a move sooner or later. I'm thinking it'll be sooner, he's got to be aware of Eamon Dunne out there, breathing fire," Dillon said.

"I want to run this past McCabe first. Just so we're covered. If O'Brien's our man, I don't want him disappearing because he copped onto us knowing that fact."

"Yeah, I suppose, but I don't want to…" Dillon's phone rang and he pulled it out without thinking. Abbey. "Shit, I've got to take this."

"I'll see you inside," Simmons said and climbed out of the car.

"Hello, Abbey."

"Don't you go sounding all nice and proper to me, ya bollocks."

"Excuse me?'

"I'll excuse you, right up your hole, you worthless plonker. Unless you've called Brianna in the last six minutes you better pray to God I don't get hold of you."

"Who?"

"Brianna," she screamed into the phone. "She's feckin' called me a dozen times today, has me driven just about demented, and all because you've been too much of a limp dick plonker to pick up the damn phone and call her. For fuck's sake. I'm absolutely ready to kill."

"I was going to call her right now," Dillon said, reaching for his wallet.

"I'll just bet you were. You can just kiss my gorgeous arse good-bye is what you can do. Wait a minute, on second thought you won't be kissing my arse or any other part of me ever again. If you think…"

"Will you please calm down? I've been working a case for the past seventy-two hours and haven't had the proper amount of time to spend on this." Dillon opened his wallet and pulled the forgotten note out. "It's Brianna, right? Her number is…" He read the number off to Abbey, and there was a long pause.

"You were really going to call her?"

"Yes. In fact I was going to call her again. I tried, oh, I don't know, maybe ten minutes ago and I got dumped into her message center, again," Dillon said, then silently prayed she'd been on the phone with this Brianna woman ten minutes ago.

"Did you leave her a message?"

Shit! "Ahh, no, I wasn't sure how secure her phone was and I was afraid someone who shouldn't know about the two of us talking might get hold of the information. Did she give you any hint what the problem was?"

"No, nothing, except that she'd only talk to you. Your man who dumped her, he's a bit of a knacker. I'm not sure what he's done, but she seemed to think it was important and wanted to talk to you."

Dillon could only imagine. She probably wanted to turn him in for lack of car insurance or taking a refill of tea without paying. "I'll call her again, right now, I promise."

"Oh thank you, it will mean a lot to her and it will get me back onto the road toward sanity. God, I wasn't kidding, I'm going to jump out the window if she calls again. Ummm, sorry if I was sort of bitchy a moment ago."

"Oh, you weren't bitchy," he lied. "I understand you being upset. I'll call her back right now, I promise."

"Then I promise I'll make it up to you."

"I'm going to hold you to that."

"Then you better rest up," she laughed, and disconnected.

Dillon looked at the note, dialed the number and hoped the infamous Brianna was on another call. She wasn't, or if she was she disconnected and answered on the third ring.

"Hello," she said, followed by a sniffle.

"Brianna, please."

"Is this the American?"

"Yeah. Hi, Brianna. Yeah this is Abbey's friend, Jack Dillon. I tried…"

"I've been waiting for almost three days, but I never heard from you."

"Gee, I tried to reach you a number of times, but I didn't want to leave a message, you know, just in case someone had access to your phone."

There was a long pause on the other end, and Dillon hoped he'd halted any Abbey-like rant before it began.

"How can I help?" he said hoping to move the conversation in a more positive direction.

# Chapter Twenty-Five

**Simmons was sitting at** his desk, in the process of dialing his phone, when he saw Dillon hurrying toward him. He placed the receiver back down and watched as he approached. "What got into you?"

"You see McCabe yet?"

He tilted his head toward McCabe's closed office door. "Top secret conference. I don't know who's in there, or what's going on. I'm guessing more heat piled on from the powers that be to solve the transit van heist and Paddy Dunne's murder. He's not going to be too happy when they leave."

"I think I've got someone who might be able to shed some light."

"What?" Simmons said, and rocked forward in his desk chair. "You gotta be shitting me."

"Come on, I'll explain on the way."

"What the hell are you talking about?" Simmons said, grabbing his key's from the desk and giving a quick look at the closed office door. They could hear raised voices emanating for the other side.

"You want to be the next one in there. I guarantee you, you'll get one hell of a warm reception. Come on," Dillon said, and hurried out the office door.

Brianna lived in an area of Dublin referred to as "The Liberties." The Guinness store house and maybe St. Patrick's Cathedral were the more notable landmarks. She lived on Ardee Street, and as it turned out, in the corner house, one of five attached units. The compact house was two stories tall, with a green front door and a sitting room window that was made up of four panes of glass and window trim painted with the same green as the door. There was a brass knocker hanging from the center of the door that looked to be at least a hundred years old.

The bricks were a rough sort of buff color with red brick trim around the window, the door and up the side corner of the house. Dillon looked up to see maybe a half-dozen blouses that appeared to be hanging from a curtain rod in front of the second floor window.

"Come on, you can look at that shite later. Let's talk to her," Simmons said. He was already ringing the doorbell while Dillon was standing in the misty evening air, looking at the structure.

"Maybe it's broken. Better use that knocker," Dillon said after they'd waited no more than five seconds.

Simmons used the knocker, rapping a half-dozen times.

"Miss Keane?" Simmons said as the front door opened a half-second later.

A heavy-set blonde woman with inch-long dark roots in hair that looked like it hadn't been washed for a week stood in the doorway. She took a long drag from a cigarette and exhaled a blue cloud up toward the second story. Her eyes were red and puffy, with dark rings of mascara giving them a haunted sort of look. She sniffled, rubbed her red, chapped nose with the handful of Kleenex she held and asked Simmons, "Are you Abbey's Jack?"

"That would be me," Dillon said, stepping alongside of Simmons. "I'm Jack Dillon, we spoke on the phone just a bit ago. This is my partner, Detective Simmons. We wanted to come over as quickly as possible to see if we could help."

"I was hoping you would have called a few days ago," she sniffled. "I don't know, it may be too late by now." She took another long drag off her cigarette, sort of blew the smoke down toward their feet, then fanned the air with a meaty hand. The evening mist was suddenly picking up a little in intensity and turning to drizzle, but she seemed not to notice.

"I wonder if we might step in and talk," Dillon said, just as three large drops fell down from the leaky roof gutter and landed on his shoulder.

Brianna just nodded, took another drag from her cigarette and stepped back into the house. Simmons and Dillon followed.

# Chapter Twenty-Six

**There was a narrow** hall in front of them with a paneled door at the darkened end. The door was blocked by a large, white plastic trash bag and an overflowing laundry basket. A narrow set of stairs just to the right featuring a banister of spindles painted white led up to the second floor. Various items were stacked in the corners of the first half-dozen steps.

Brianna waddled through an open door on the left and into a small sitting room. Two over-stuffed, brown, faux-leather couches faced one another with a tinted glass coffee table between them. The arms on both couches were worn, and the coffee table had a crack in the glass running across the width of the table.

Arrangements of framed photos hung on two walls, but it looked like four or five of the frames had recently been removed. A number of photos were stacked on the cushion of a corner chair. A pair of scissors rested on top of the photos, and it appeared that something or someone had been cut out of each image.

A near-empty, open bottle of Jameson sat at the far end of the coffee table. A lamp with a dim light sat on the end table alongside the couch, and a box of Kleenex rested next to the lamp.

Brianna set her cigarette in a large, overflowing ashtray, picked up a glass and took a healthy swallow of what Dillon presumed was Jameson. He noticed her fingernail polish was black. He was suddenly aware of Leonard Cohen playing softly in the background from somewhere. "Depressing" was the word that sprang immediately to mind.

She took another sip from her glass, but didn't bother to offer Dillon or Simmons any. Once she swallowed she wiped her lips using her hand that held the glass, took a deep breath, sighed and said, "I suppose you heard he dumped me?"

"Actually, that's about all we know," Dillon said. "Abbey didn't tell me anything else, said she wanted to respect your privacy."

"Oh, isn't she a dear. But I don't know why she'd bother? By now just about every knacker in the Liberties knows he took me for the royal ride. Literally. Then the bastard just kicked me to the side of the road," she said with a shrug suggesting no one would be surprised.

"And you mentioned just a bit over the phone. Why did he do this? What happened? I thought you two were the perfect couple," Dillon lied.

She took another sip. "Weren't you listening? He found another ride and the bollocks is all of a sudden in the money. Told me he was making one big withdrawal from Slándáil Transit where he works, and that was gonna take care of him for the rest of his life, him and that slapper Noreen Dempsey." She took another sip of whiskey in an effort to wash Noreen's name from her lips.

"She'll take him for all he's got and more. Good riddance to the both of them is all I can say." She sniffled, reached for a Kleenex, loudly blew her reddened, chapped nose, into the Kleenex, then dropped it onto the pile next to her feet before she reached for her glass.

"When did he tell you this?"

She drained her glass, swallowed and sighed. "Three, no, wait, I guess it would be maybe four nights ago now. That plonker's been riding me regular like for going on two years, and suddenly I ain't good enough for him anymore."

"And this is Tommy O'Brien you're talking about?" Simmons asked.

"Might be." Brianna suddenly seemed to sit up a little straighter. "Before I tell you anymore, I'd want your assurances I'm not going to be prosecuted. I don't need the likes of you arresting me. I still got my pride, or what's left of it. I need to hear it from the both of yas."

"Assurances, yes, sure, of course. You're not going to be prosecuted, you're aiding in our investigation," Simmons said.

"I just want to help in whatever way we can, Brianna. Don't want to arrest you. For God's sake, we'd never do such a thing," Dillon said.

"I'd need my involvement kept a secret. Your man that was killed, that was Eamon Dunne's brother, wasn't it?"

They both nodded.

"That bastard won't be sitting still for it. Someone's going to pay, and I don't want it to be the likes of me."

"I promise, give my word," Simmons said, raising his hand as if he was taking an oath in court. "You said this is Tommy O'Brien we're talking about?"

"Jesus! Who the hell else?" she said, then proceeded to empty the Jameson bottle into her glass. The remnants barely covered the bottom of her glass. "Shite," she groaned, and set the empty bottle on the floor.

"Can you describe him to us?"

She looked at Simmons for a brief moment. "Describe him? I can do better than that, I can show you pictures. Just in case you don't believe me, I got a trash bin out in the back crammed full of the bastard's clothes and shoes," she said.

She leaned forward and forced a hand into the back pocket of her tight-fitting jeans. It looked like there wouldn't be room for a dime back there, let alone the sparkling pink cellphone she pulled out.

"This good enough for the likes of yas," she said, running a finger across the screen of her cellphone to unlock it. She quickly clicked on a number of different buttons using both her thumbs. "Here, how's this for your damn identification?" she said and thrust the cellphone toward Simmons. He stared at the screen for a long moment, then passed it over to Dillon.

There it was, a couple's selfie, the two of them in a coital embrace. Brianna with her back to the mirror, her legs wrapped around Tommy and holding the phone. Tommy O'Brien facing the mirror, looking like he was working diligently. There was a white arrowhead in the middle of the image suggesting it was a video. Dillon really didn't feel the need to set the image in motion.

"I wonder if you wouldn't mind if we hung onto your phone," Simmons said.

"As a matter of fact, I certainly would mind. I've got your number here, Dillon. I'll just send them to you, along with the photos. I got a mess of them. Just give me a minute?"

"Do you know where Tommy is now?" Simmons asked just as Dillon's cellphone alerted him to a message coming in.

"He's at the Shelbourne," she said, busily working both thumbs on the screen of her phone. "The fecker, never, ever brought the likes of me there, told me the other night he was always too embarrassed, didn't want to be seen with my arse on his arm. The bastard. He'll be there with his fancy, important American friend, and herself, that Dempsey bitch, the slapper."

"American friend?" Dillon asked just as his phone pinged two more times.

"And you're the one supposed to have the great mind?" She gave Dillon a questioning look. "He's the brains behind the Slándáil Transit hit. Don't think for a moment that shite-for-brains Tommy could come up with the plan."

132

"Would you remember his name?" Dillon asked and held his breath.

"He just called him Eddie. I only seen your man once, that was the night Tommy dumped me. The night before the robbery. Bastard was out on the street, sitting in his fancy car, honked the horn for him and Tommy just walked out the door as calm as could be. Never once looked back or said sorry or thank you or see ya later or to hell with yas. He just dumped me," she said, then began to quietly sob.

Dillon's phone pinged again.

After a long moment she reached alongside the couch, pulled up an unopened bottle of Jameson and set it on the coffee table.

"Brianna, I want you to know you've been an awfully big help. More help than you'll ever realize," Simmons said. "Based on what you told us we have to hurry, but we'll be in touch. I'm going to make a call and have a car parked outside your door, just so you're safe. When you see it out there, don't worry. He's there to protect you. Once we have Tommy arrested and everything locked down, we'll let you know it's safe. Okay?"

Brianna cracked the seal on the bottle of Jameson, and was in the process of pouring her glass a good two-thirds full. "Whatever. I ain't going nowhere," she said, then set the bottle down and took a long sip. "You's can let yourself out? I'll be sending you more of them images. Be a pleasure to nail the wanker's bum to the wall. See what he thinks of dumping me then."

133

"Thanks, Brianna. We'll be in touch," Dillon said, then bent down and kissed her on the forehead. She was in desperate need of a shower and probably some heavy-duty psychiatric care as well. She didn't react, just sat there on the couch, staring at the whiskey glass in her hand with tears rolling down her cheeks. Leonard Cohen groaned from somewhere in the background.

They walked out of the room, and Dillon's phone pinged just as they got to the front door. It pinged two more times before they made it to the car.

"God, how many of those shots does she have?"

"A reminder to us all," Simmons said, "Hell hath no fury like a woman scorned."

"Safest place for Tommy O'Brien right now might just be locked up in prison. She almost makes your man Eamon Dunne pale in comparison."

# Chapter Twenty-Seven

**"I fucking knew it,"** Simmons half-screamed as he put his cellphone up to his ear. "It just wasn't fitting, didn't add up. Then your lads this afternoon. Saying he refused any medical attention, with the blood all over him. Telling them to work on Paddy Dunne, poor bastard already dead and that stupid fucking bastard… What? Oh sorry, no sir, not you," Simmons said, shaking his head like he couldn't believe what just happened.

"I think we just got the break we've been looking for. The first thing we're going to need is an around the clock presence at a home in the Liberties, on Ardee Street. I need someone parked outside the front door for protection. We believe your man is as bold as can be and staying at the Shelbourne. No, sir, I'm serious, right out in the open. You might try the American's name first, Fleming, Eddie or Edward, maybe check for your man Tommy O'Brien next. Yes, that Tommy O'Brien. We've a strong suspicion he's going to make an appearance tonight at Kennedy's. We're heading there to meet him now."

He paused and listened for a long moment, then viciously kicked at some imaginary item in front of him. "I really don't want to wait, sir." Simmons suddenly flashed a look and shook his head.

"What?" Dillon whispered.

He mouthed the word "fuck" then said, "Very well, sir, we'll wait, but I don't want to wait too long. You know how things have a habit of...Yes, sir, we're just ten, maybe fifteen minutes away. Very good," Simmons said, disconnected and then swore a blue streak.

"Problem?"

"Bloody hell. The bollocks wants us to wait until backup arrives. God save us. Come on, let's get over to Kennedy's before they page your man to come to the bar to be arrested by the Garda and he ducks out the side door."

They ran two red lights and scared the hell out of countless drivers. When he wasn't flashing his headlights or honking the horn, Simmons was cursing at cars to get out of his way.

"It's only half past eight, he probably hasn't had time to even finish his first pint. I'll lay you odds he phoned a bunch of people and set up some sort of hero's welcome for himself," Dillon said.

"I'm just worried if he catches on, or Fleming learns of this he'll contact O'Brien, they'll go to ground, and that'll be the end of it. I'll just feel better when we've the both of them under arrest and locked up. God save us, but it just wasn't adding up. I knew it wasn't making sense. I fecking knew it."

It was about a fifteen-minute drive to Kennedy's. Dillon figured they made it in less than eight minutes. They had to wait for some big dark-blue car to take its time making a right-hand turn before they could pull onto the side street and park. As the car turned, it sounded like a strange thumping was coming from the rear. Simmons parked directly in front of a fire hydrant and hurried out of the car before Dillon was even unbuckled. "Come on, I want to get in there as soon as our backup arrives," Simmons called, heading for the corner. Dillon had to trot to catch up as they hurried around the corner toward Kennedy's.

The pub was on Westland Row, sitting in the first floor corner of a three-story brick building. The place had a red stone exterior with black trim, and as you faced it there were actually two doors, one on either end, going into the place. One door was labeled "Bar," the other labeled "Lounge."

Dillon positioned himself against the wall of the "Lounge" door, hoping to look like one of the patrons just killing time, maybe waiting for a pal or a date. Simmons did the same alongside the "Bar" door at the corner of the building.

An advertisement blackboard was positioned on the sidewalk with colored chalk letters advertising Galway Hooker beer and baked ham sandwiches. Neither one of them had eaten anything other than the subway sandwich they'd split, for the better part of the day, and Dillon was suddenly starving. They waited there for the next twenty minutes. Occasionally someone would step outside to smoke a cigarette, but never anyone who looked the least bit like Tommy O'Brien. Simmons was on his phone twice, involved in an animated conversation with some poor soul. Finally, two guys came around the corner, stopped and spoke with Simmons briefly. After a moment he turned and hurried down the sidewalk to where Dillon was waiting.

"Everything okay?" Dillon asked.

"We're about to find out," Simmons said, not looking at all happy. "We'll go in and look around. When we see him we'll just suggest we want a private word. Get him to go out calmly. Maybe suggest we want to give him protection in the event the robbers come looking for him. That sound good to you?"

"Yeah, I suppose, unless he wonders what in the hell we're doing here in the first place. Maybe tell him we got word someone is searching for him without mentioning names. If he's as crooked as we think, he'll be afraid Eamon Dunne figured things out and he's screwed if he doesn't go with us."

"Well, the key is to get him to come calmly outside with us. We'll figure it out. All right, in we go," Simmons said, sounding more than a little impatient. He gave a wave to the two men at the far end down by the "Bar" door, and they all headed into Kennedy's at the same time.

Simmons and Dillon entered via the "Lounge" door. The lounge turned out to be a compact room with a wooden floor, an arched wooden ceiling and a fireplace with a mirror advertising "Kennedy's Whiskey Bonder and Merchants" in large gold letters. The walls on either side of the fireplace were a sort of purplish burgundy, depending on the light, and the other walls were painted a gold sort of tone. The tables were fairly close together, and over in the far corner sat a group of eight or ten guys. They were seated around two tables that had been pushed together. They were laughing quite a bit and looked to be enjoying themselves.

They occasionally clinked glasses in a toast, and their voices, while not shouting, suggested they weren't on their first pints. One or two of them gave the new arrivals, Simmons and Dillon, a quick glance, but didn't seem to pay any heed as the two of them stood scanning the room.

Tommy O'Brien was nowhere to be seen. They took a second look at everyone in the room, but he definitely wasn't there. They turned to walk into the bar just as the other two guys were heading toward the lounge from the bar. One of them held his hands at his sides, palms up, indicating they hadn't seen O'Brien.

"One of yas check the loo," Simmons said, then turned and frantically triple-checked everyone in the lounge. "Go into the bar area, Dillon, see if you can spot the bastard," he said.

Dillon walked into the bar area. There were black and white tiles on the floor, a good-sized bar with stools, and glass shelves behind the bar holding bottles of liquor. Beveled mirrors lined the walls behind the bottles and reflected their images. The lights were bright, people were chatting and laughing, and Tommy O'Brien was nowhere to be found.

The guy who'd gone to check the loo suddenly stepped back through a door with a questioning look on his face, shaking his head.

"I checked 'em both, mens and ladies,'" he said just as a woman hurried over to a table and launched into an animated conversation with the other people at the table, occasionally pointing at the apparent ladies' room intruder.

His partner suddenly stepped into the bar area and waved the two of them back into the lounge. Simmons was addressing the crowd of guys sitting back in the far corner. The rest of the room was quickly growing silent.

"… concerned for his safety and wanted to get him somewhere we'll be able to protect him. Not a reflection on you lot, but we need to know where he is, for his own protection."

"He said they'd just be a minute."

"Big plonker," one of them added.

"Had a shaved head, and a nose that sort of spread across his face," another said, running his fingers across his cheekbones.

Simmons looked at Dillon, mouthed the word "Mousey" and shook his head. "Thanks for your time, lads," he said, then passed business cards around while trying not to sound too stressed out. "If he comes back, have him give me a call. We just want to make sure he's all right after all he's been through," he said, then indicated the door with a wave of his hand.

Once outside they gathered in a tight little group, glanced up and down in the forlorn hope they'd see

Tommy O'Brien either sitting outside or heading toward them.

"Apparently he stepped out with someone who wanted to talk to him. Sounded like that bastard Mousey from Slándáil Transit. And if he was here…" Simmons pressed a speed dial button on his cellphone and put the phone to his ear. "…that can only mean one thing. Eamon Dunne."

"It's Simmons, sir. He's not here. We just missed him." He shot a look at the two guys they'd spent twenty minutes waiting for. "No, we're thinking maybe Eamon Dunne. The description fit one of his underlings. No, sir. Apparently someone came in, spoke to him for a moment, and he left, saying he'd be right back, only he never came back. I've no idea, sir. Anything on Eddie Fleming? Yes, if you would, sir. Thank you," he said, and disconnected.

"They're about to head into the Shelbourne. I don't know, maybe Dildo and I head over there, see if O'Brien shows up. You two might as well stay here just in case he returns." Simmons didn't sound all that positive.

Once in the car he just shook his head. "We missed him, waiting for those two plonkers to show up. Damn it."

"I don't know that we can blame them. If he was there while we were waiting, he would have come out of one of the doors and we'd have seen him," Dillon said. "That description they gave sure seemed to fit Mousey."

"For all the good it'll do," Simmons said, then turned the key and pulled away from the curb.

"You think Brianna might have contacted Eamon Dunne?" Dillon asked.

Simmons glanced over at him. "I think anything is possible at this point. Although she seemed frightened enough by the prospect of him ever finding out. I'm willing to bet she kept her mouth shut, trouble is we don't know about everyone else."

# Chapter Twenty-Eight

**They were just a** few minutes from the Shelbourne Hotel, and met McCabe and five others in the lobby. The hotel was a six-story building overlooking St. Stephen's Green, with a five-star rating, and if you have to ask how much a room costs you wouldn't be able to afford it to begin with. Not exactly where you'd expect a guy who had just pulled off a robbery and killed someone in the process to hide out, even if the robbery garnered two-point-five million, but then again...

McCabe was off to the side, talking to someone in a grey suit, starched white shirt and a striped tie who didn't look all that happy.

"That's the manager," one of the guys said. "Not all that excited with us being here."

They chatted on for a few more minutes, the manager occasionally shaking his head no. Finally they shook hands and McCabe stepped over to the group. "We'll be heading into the Heritage wing, that's where their suite is located. They ask that we remain quiet and not attract attention," McCabe said, and looked from face to face.

"We don't wish to disturb any guests. Mr. Jennings, the manager on duty, has been gracious enough to accompany us." He smiled in a way that suggested this maybe wasn't the best of news. "All right, let's be off, and quietly, please, quietly," he cautioned as if he were speaking to grammar school students.

They followed the manager en masse across the elegant lobby. No one gave them a second look, probably thinking they were simply a group of salesmen from across the EU, seeing all of Dublin in a day. They walked through a set of double doors with beveled glass and down a wide, elegant hallway. Oil paintings of Dublin scenes surrounded by gilt frames hung from the wall. Jennings, the manager, stopped at one point, turned and put a finger to his lips even though no one had spoken a word since they had stepped off in the lobby. "Just around the corner," he half-whispered. "I'll knock on the door and announce."

They went another fifteen feet or so, then turned left and entered a small alcove. They watched as Jennings knocked on the door. As he knocked, McCabe placed a finger over the peephole in the door just as Jennings called out, "Hotel management."

Jennings looked at him, and McCabe just shook his head. Jennings knocked on the door once again, this time saying, "Mr. Fleming, hotel management." McCabe's finger remained in place.

The two of them had a brief discussion a moment later, McCabe and Jennings, and then Jennings inserted a pass card in the slot on the door, opened the door, stepped aside, and everyone swarmed past him. "Excuse me, Mr. Fleming? Hotel management," Jennings called as they spread through the suite.

The suite was elegant with a large sitting room, two bedrooms and three bathrooms, all of it over looking St. Stephen's Green. Two off-white couches sat facing one another with an elegant coffee table in between. There were matted and framed watercolors on the wall, a live white orchid on the windowsill, and no Eddie Fleming. Everyone knew they were too late almost the moment they stepped inside.

The two couches were neatly arranged in front of a gas fireplace with a small fire glowing behind glass doors. A table rested against the wall opposite the fireplace. What had once been an elegant, large, gold-framed mirror hung on the wall above the table. The chair that had been in front of the table lay on its side. The large mirror was now hanging at an odd angle and had a series of cracks in a spider-web pattern along one side. A trickle of congealed blood ran down the glass and collected in a small puddle along the heavy gold frame. A crystal vase lay shattered on the floor alongside the table, and maybe two dozen red tulips littered the floor. The door frame leading into the larger of the two bedrooms was bloodied.

The attached bathroom had a Jacuzzi tub, still filled with water, and a container of bubble bath resting on a marble shelf. Next to the bubble bath was a crystal glass with just a swallow of whiskey remaining and a trace of lipstick around the edge of the glass. A bottle of

Connemara whiskey with maybe just an inch remaining rested on the floor next to the Jacuzzi. A woman's under garments rested on the bathroom's white marble vanity top.

Perhaps even more telling, two, crisp hundred euro notes lay on the carpet on the far side of the four-poster bed.

Two suitcases, one black and worn, the other a Louis Vuitton, were open and full of clothes. Off to the side on the window sill was what at first Dillon thought might be a cat. Upon closer examination it turned out to be a grey wig. On the floor below it was a dark dress and an old-fashioned woman's hat.

The second bedroom appeared to be untouched except for another worn black bag sitting on the dresser.

McCabe hustled everyone out of the suite. Simmons and Dillon lingered by the door.

"He was here," Dillon said. "Son of a bitch, Fleming was here. I'll lay you odds that's his luggage in there, and Tommy O'Brien's and some slapper's in the other room."

"It had to be Eamon Dunne," Simmons said.

McCabe seemed to think for a moment then said, "All right, out of here, the two of ye. I'll want forensics in here right away."

Once outside on the street, Simmons looked at Dillon and just shook his head. They stood looking at one another like two stalled vehicles in the middle of a six-lane highway with people walking past, in a hurry, with purpose to their steps, going to wherever they were headed.

"Well, we've got a lead on Eamon Dunne's guy, Mousey. He was at Kennedy's, they can identify him. They basically said he went in there, said something to Tommy O'Brien and the two of them left together."

"They won't identify him," Simmons said, shaking his head. "They'd be crazy to do so."

"That car we had to wait for, just before you parked and we went into Kennedy's, the one with the thumping in the back, that could have been Dunne's Mercedes."

"It could have been the Pope, too. You're grasping at straws. Your man Dunne's grabbed all three of them, I'm guessing along with two-point-five million euros."

"Certainly we can bring him in for questioning?"

Simmons looked at Dillon like he didn't get it, and maybe he didn't.

"I suppose we could bring them in tomorrow and question…"

"Tomorrow? Let's bring them in tonight, find them, check Dunne's home, find out where…"

"Tomorrow, Jack. Can I drop you somewhere?" Simmons' tone suggested there was no point in going on, or trying to push.

"You sure? We could…"

"You need a ride or not?"

"Yeah, my car's back at the office."

"Come on, I'll give you a lift," Simmons said, and headed down the street to where they'd parked.

# Chapter Twenty-Nine

**The following morning they** attempted to contact Eamon Dunne along with his employee Malcolm Hardy, aka Mousey, hoping they'd join them for some polite conversation. Perhaps not surprisingly, hours before Tommy O'Brien was discharged from the hospital, both men had left the country for a short vacation in France. They traveled on a chartered flight departing from Weston Airport and returned from France five days later.

Eamon Dunne graciously responded to the requests upon his return. Mousey agreed to join them once they sent two Garda cars and four officers around to bring him in. Both men were armed with receipts documenting their trip, hotel stay, dinners, tours and a nice bottle of wine that each man presented to McCabe.

McCabe had them placed in separate rooms for the interview. Neither man spoke until their legal counsel arrived, and then once they began, both interviews were concluded within the hour.

"That's it, they can just walk?" Dillon asked McCabe. They'd watched the two of them, Dunne and

Mousey, walk out of the building, slapping one another on the back and laughing. Dillon was still seething, sitting now in McCabe's office with the door closed. McCabe seemed to be exhaling a number of long cleansing breaths in an apparent attempt to remain calm. Under the circumstances, Dillon didn't feel his questions were helping.

"According to the documentation," McCabe said, "they left the country together, in the early afternoon, and remained in France for the past five days until their return yesterday. They both forgot to bring their cellphones and left them in the office by mistake."

"You can't believe that, come on. We spoke to eye witnesses who saw Mousey get Tommy O'Brien out of Kennedy's the night he disappeared. They described him perfectly, for Christ sake."

"Yes, and all three witnesses have since come in and signed statements that they were tragically mistaken." McCabe grabbed the signed statements from the corner of his desk and casually tossed them across toward Dillon.

"They couldn't identify this Mousey bastard from the mug shots we showed them. They were adamant that they'd been mistaken." McCabe held his hands open in a pose that suggested, "What do you want me to do?"

"But that night at Kennedy's, they described him, Mousey. They mentioned his nose and the shaved head and…"

"And they've now stated that they were horribly mistaken."

"How can anyone be in two places at once, Kennedy's pub and, at the same time, France?"

"Perhaps you weren't listening. According to the revised statement, your man Mousey wasn't in Kennedy's pub. Both their passports have been documented arriving in France."

"Did you check the stamps?"

McCabe smiled, "It's the EU, there are no stamps for citizens."

"What about the receipts? They could have…"

"They both used their credit cards, or paid cash." He folded his hands, slowly closed his eyes, then opened them again and looked at Dillon.

"What they probably did is give the pilot and two other idiots a free vacation for five days," Dillon said.

"Probably. Will there be anything else, Marshal Dillon?"

"So this is it? The investigation ends here?"

"For the moment."

# <u>Chapter Thirty</u>

**Three days later a** BMW that had been rented to Eddie Fleming was found in the Dublin Mountains. Three bodies had been crammed in the trunk. Forty-eight hours later, Dillon was at the Dublin morgue in viewing room three, again, waiting for McCabe and Simmons to show up. A shade was pulled down over the viewing window. Even though there was the constant noise of a fan in the ceiling air ducts, he'd been in the room for a good five minutes and still couldn't get used to the pine smell. It was so strong his eyes felt as though they were about to water.

Suddenly the door opened and McCabe and Simmons entered.

"Waiting long?" Simmons asked.

"I don't know, I'm damn near light-headed from the disinfectant or whatever that pine smell is."

A moment later the shade was pulled up and the same dark-haired beauty with piercing blue eyes who'd given them Paddy Dunne's autopsy report wheeled a gurney up against the window. "What's her name, Simmons?" Dillon whispered.

"Alicia, Alicia Byrne. Nice isn't it?"

"Quiet you two," McCabe said, then gave a nod, and she pulled back the sheet covering the face. It was Tommy O'Brien, or what was left of him.

"Jesus Christ," Dillon whispered.

He was missing an eye. His nose was pushed over to the far side of his face. He sported a major gash across the top of his skull. His mouth and lower jaw appeared to rest at an odd angle. Half of one ear was missing. In general, he looked like he'd had a pretty tough go of it.

McCabe nodded, said, "Thomas O'Brien." Alicia nodded, then pulled the sheet back over his face and wheeled the gurney off to the side. Someone appeared from behind, pushing another gurney in place alongside the window, then stepped over and pulled the gurney with Tommy O'Brien's body out the door.

McCabe nodded to Alicia, then half-turned and looked at Dillon. She deftly pulled the white sheet away from the face, and Dillon was suddenly looking at Eddie Fleming. His normally bright blue eyes looked flat, almost plastic. He apparently didn't suffer the beating that Tommy O'Brien had, but there was an obvious hole in the middle of his forehead, maybe a half-inch above his left eyebrow. So much for his escape from federal prison.

"That's him, Eddie Fleming," Dillon said.

McCabe nodded, and Alicia pushed Eddie's gurney off to the side, then turned as a third gurney was rolled up alongside the window. The same guy who removed Tommy's body from the room now wheeled Eddie Fleming back out the door.

McCabe gave his nod, and Alicia deftly pulled back the pressed sheet and looked up at the three of them. A woman who might have once been attractive, in a slutty sort of way, stared blankly up at the ceiling through swollen eyes. Her bleached-blonde hair was almost white, and trimmed short. Although the sheet covered her up to the shoulders it was obvious she was large breasted and Dillon recalled Tommy O'Brien's comment the first time he and Simmons had interviewed him, 'She had a nice set on her.'

Dillon noticed the one earlobe he could see was slit, and purple, as if the pierced earring had been yanked out. Her nose was swollen and discolored, most likely broken at some point. Her purple and swollen lips were parted, and from what Dillon could see her teeth had been knocked or pulled out. McCabe and Simmons slowly shook their heads.

"No idea," said McCabe.

"Never seen her," Simmons said.

Dillon certainly had no idea, then remembered something Brianna had said the night he and Simmons and had talked with her.

"I can't ID her, but check out someone named Noreen Dempsey. She lives, or lived, somewhere in the Liberties," he said.

McCabe looked at him.

153

"Just something someone mentioned. Rumor on the street was a woman by that name had taken up with Tommy O'Brien."

McCabe nodded. Alicia covered the woman's face with the sheet and pulled the shade down. They quickly escaped the pine smell by heading out through the front office.

"Well," McCabe said, standing outside on the front steps. "That would seem to bring one part of the investigation closed and open up three additional avenues. And we're still no closer to the stolen funds."

"Ahh, Jaysus," Simmons groaned. "Eamon Dunne is sitting on that, just as pretty as you please."

"Unless he sent it back to France with whoever went over there pretending to be him for five days," Dillon said.

The two of them looked at him and just shook their heads, then McCabe said, "All right, back to the office with you, Dildo. Think you can find your way?"

# <u>Epilogue</u>

**They were in Dillon's** sitting room, Lucifer, Abbey and Dillon. Dillon had the drapes pulled and had just opened their second bottle of wine. Abbey was feeding Lucifer crackers and cheese when she thought Dillon wasn't looking. She was facing Dillon on the couch, wearing a very short skirt with her legs tucked beneath her. Her red heels rested on the floor. She was wearing some sort of stretch top that was indeed stretched, displaying substantial cleavage and leaving nothing to the imagination.

"Do you still think I'm a bitch?"

"No, Abbey, I don't. I never thought that. If we'd gotten to Brianna sooner we might have been able to save all three of them. I just, well, it never dawned on me that her being dumped related to the case we were working on."

"No loss on that slapper, Noreen. She's gone for someones man before, it was like a hot button for her. The guy was supposed to be taken so she was gonna prove he'd still give her a ride. A right pain in the hole, that one is. Or, well, I guess was." She took a sip of wine, then set her glass down on the coffee table.

Dillon reached for the wine bottle and topped up her glass.

"Trying to get me plastered, are ye?"

"No, just trying to get you in the mood."

155

"Relax, I'm in the mood and I know, I haven't forgotten, I said I'd make it worth your while."

"If only I'd talked to her sooner."

"It worked out okay for her. She's better off without that bollocks. Tommy O'Brien got what was coming to him. Don't you go feeling sorry for that plonker."

"Would have been nice to see him stand trial and just go to prison."

"Yeah, and then Eamon Dunne just would have had him killed in there."

"Yeah, but if…" Lucifer suddenly barked, and a moment later the doorbell rang. "Jesus, what the hell time is it?" Dillon said and looked at his watch. It was almost ten.

He got up from the couch just as the doorbell rang again. He stepped out into the front hall and turned on the outside light. There was a man standing out there, holding what seemed to be a fairly large package. He looked like he might be wearing a dark-blue baseball cap and was dressed in some sort of dark-blue uniform, although it was next to impossible to tell peering through the door's decorative glass panel.

Dillon opened the door just as Abbey called from the sitting room, "Don't open the door."

"Hi, Mr. Dillon?" the man said. He held a large package, maybe three feet by five feet, wrapped in white paper. Behind him out on the street was a dark-blue van, square, heavy-looking, solid and with the words "Slándáil Transit" in yellow letters with a red shadow painted along the side of the van.

"Yeah?"

"Sorry for the late hour delivery. A gift sir, from Mr. Eamon Dunne. May I?" he said, then indicated the large package and the door.

"What? Oh, yeah, sure, I guess so. Sorry about that. Ahh, just bring it in the hallway here and you can lean it up against the wall," Dillon said, then stepped aside.

The man reached down, picked up a bottle of wine and handed it to Dillon then stepped into the front hall, set the package carefully against the far wall just as Abbey appeared in the sitting room doorway.

"This is from Eamon Dunne?" Dillon asked examining the bottle.

"French wine, no doubt very expensive and the best available."

"What's all this for?" Dillon asked.

"Sorry, sir, I haven't the faintest idea. I'm just the delivery man." He looked over and stared at Abbey for a moment, ogled her revealing top and the short skirt almost not covering her. She held a glass of wine in her hand, smiled, and her eyes seemed to take on a sparkle.

"Enjoy your evening, sir," he said, then sort of waved a hand off the bill of his cap, stepped out the door and headed for the Slándáil Transit van without bothering to look back.

Dillon closed the door behind him and turned to face a wide-eyed Abbey.

"The likes of Eamon Dunne sent you a bottle of wine and a present? Come on now, don't keep me guessing, go ahead and open it up."

"I'm not sure I want to."

"Oh for feck's sake. Here, hold this," she said, thrusting her wine glass toward Dillon. She stepped over to the package and pulled it away from the wall. "It's a bit heavy, feels kind of solid." She carefully began to remove the white paper while Lucifer stood alongside her, sniffing the package.

"God, it's heavy. Maybe it's like an expensive painting or something," she said, as she began to rip the paper off, obviously in a hurry to see what lay behind. "I bet it's a...Oh, God, I mean it's, it's nice and all, I guess, but did you? You know, did you want this?"

Dillon looked at the heavy gold frame around the shiny mirror. The mirror from Eddie Flemings room at the Shelbourne, now repaired, or maybe just one very much like it, brand new. The spider-web smash on the right hand side was gone, and there wasn't the stream of blood down the glass or pooled along the bottom of the frame.

"It's really beautiful, I guess." Abbey turned to look at Dillon, grabbed her glass, took a large sip of wine and said, "God, imagine, Eamon Dunne himself. He must really like you."

## The End

Thank you for taking the time to read <u>Mirror Mirror</u>, the third tale in the Jack Dillon Dublin series. If you enjoyed the read please consider leaving a review on Amazon, it really helps. Don't miss the list of all my books on the following pages. Thanks…

# Books by Mike Faricy

*The following titles are stand alone;*

Baby Grand
Chow For Now
Slow, Slow, Quick, Quick
Merlot
Finders Keepers
End of the Line

Irish Dukes (Fight Card Series)
*written under the pseudonym Jack Tunney*

All the stand alone titles are
available on Amazon.

*The following titles comprise the Dev Haskell series;*

Russian Roulette: Case 1
Mr. Swirlee: Case 2
Bite Me: Case 3
Bombshell: Case 4
Tutti Frutti: Case 5
Last Shot: Case 6
Ting-A-Ling: Case 7
Crickett: Case 8
Bulldog: Case 9
Double Trouble: Case 10
Yellow Ribbon: Case 11
Dog Gone: Case 12
Scam Man: Case 13
Foiled: Case 14
What Happens in Vegas… : Case 15
Art Hound: Case 16
The Office: Case 17

*The following titles are Dev Haskell novellas;*
Dollhouse
The Dance
Pixie
*Fore!*

Twinkle Toes
(*a Dev Haskell short story*)

The Dev Haskell series is available on Amazon.

*The following titles comprise
the Corridor Man series
written under the pseudonym
Nick James;*

Corridor Man
Corridor Man 2: Opportunity knocks
Corridor Man 3: The Dungeon
Corridor Man 4: Dead End
Corridor Man 5: Finger
Corridor Man 6: Exit Strategy
Corridor Man 7: Trunk Music
*Corridor Man novellas;*
Corridor Man: Valentine
Corridor Man: Auditor
Corridor Man: Howling


The Corridor Man series
is available on Amazon.

*The following titles comprise the Jack Dillon Dublin Tales series written under the pseudonym Patrick Emmett.*

Welcome
*Jack Dillon Dublin Tale 1*

Sweet Dreams
*Jack Dillon Dublin Tale 2*

Mirror Mirror
*Jack Dillon Dublin Tale 3*

Silver Bullet
*Jack Dillon Dublin Tale 4*

Fair City Blues
*Jack Dillon Dublin Tale 5*

The Jack Dillon Dublin Tales series is available on Amazon.

Contact Mike;
Email: mikefaricyauthor@gmail.com
Twitter: @Mikefaricybooks
Facebook: DevHaskell or
MikeFaricyBooks
Website: http://
www.mikefaricybooks.com

# Thank you!

Made in the USA
Middletown, DE
21 July 2021